The Vitae

A Rose Brashear Novella

Lesann Berry

Isinglass Press
SILVERLAKE, WASHINGTON

Isinglass Press
PO Box 1731
Castle Rock, WA 98611
www.isinglasspress.com

Publisher's Note: This is a work of fiction. Names, characters, places, and incidents are a product of the author's imagination. Locales and public names are sometimes used for atmospheric purposes. Any resemblance to actual people, living or dead, or to businesses, companies, events, institutions, or locales is completely coincidental.

Cover Design by Carrie Spencer at www.cheekycovers.com
Interior Design by www.BookDesignTemplates.com

Ordering Information:
Quantity sales. Special discounts are available on quantity purchases by corporations, associations, and others. For details, contact the "Special Sales Department" at the address above.

The Vitae / Lesann Berry. -- 1st ed.
ISBN 978-1-939316-07-3

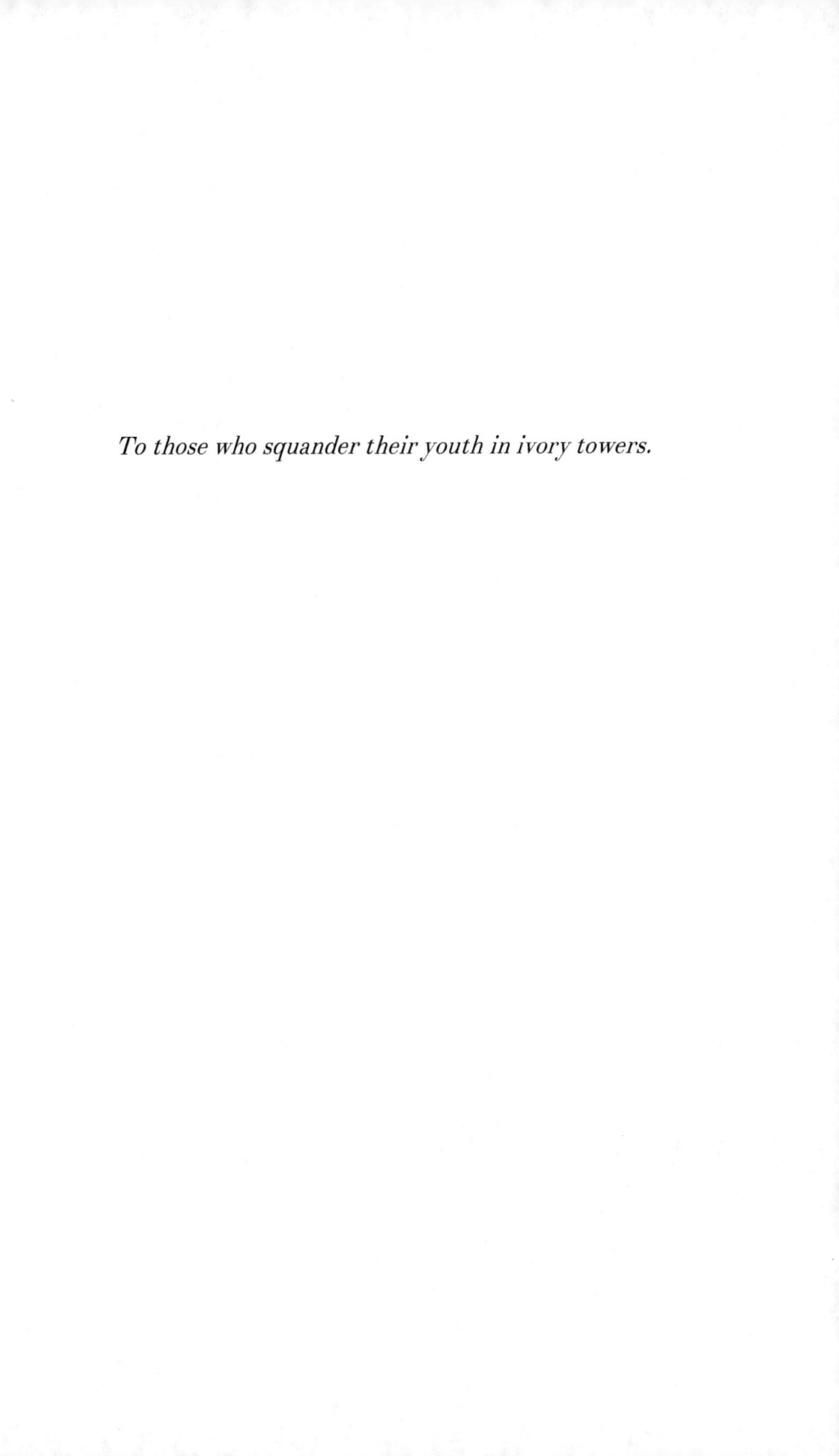

To those who squander their youth in ivory towers.

The un-attempted remains impossible.

—ANONYMOUS

CHAPTER ONE

The Memo

Rose Brashear dragged the sheaf of papers from her faculty mailbox slot and staggered over to drop her shoulder pack on the copy machine. The small room which served the anthropology division might feature the typical drab institutional decor but it successfully doubled as an echo chamber. She rubbed at the tender muscle where the strap from her bulging khaki bag had dug a furrow into the soft tissue between her neck and clavicle. Blocking the thick stack of student research proposals from spilling out of the top, she tugged the bag into a more upright position.

The introductory anthropology class was her favorite course to teach because the curriculum offered a brief look at the main subfields of the discipline. She loved that she got to share the most exciting parts of her profession. The wide array of specializations which made anthropology such a diverse field also made the discipline a viable minor for almost any major. She couldn't wait to get home later this afternoon, pull on some sweats and crank up the heater, before opening a bottle of red wine and start reading.

Utilizing the top surface of the copy machine, she tapped the stack of mail into a neat pile, her eyes scanning the cover of a catalog featuring DVDs pertinent to her field. The air in the room was stale and cold, the scent of toner from the recent equipment service layered on a wet chemical note. Her stomach growled and she remembered the banana she'd crammed inside her bag this morning. Darting out the door, later than usual, she'd grabbed the fruit as an emergency ration. The last granola bar she'd fished out of the back of her desk drawer had been hard as a brick and might date back to her sophomore year when she'd been recruited to clean Dr. Wilcox's office. This was her extra-long day on campus and she should have remembered to pack a lunch, another plan sideswiped by a late night with a good novel. She raised one hand, ready to plunge inside the bag when Thelma Chen darted through the door.

The senior graduate assistant flapped her arm at the copier. "Don't get comfortable, Rose. I've got eight minutes to make fifty copies of this quiz and beat feet down three flights of stairs before Dr. Edgestein drags his ass to class."

Rose shifted sideways and spilled her pile of stuff on the neighboring stack of boxes. "I'm definitely Team Thelma."

Dr. Edgestein was the least favorite of the senior faculty. He delighted in making life difficult for his graduate assistants and his reputation as a world-renowned scholar guaranteed an endless supply of willing sacrifices. Rose thought he was a jerk. When he'd selected Thelma from the list of candidates last summer, he'd underestimated the tiger inside the slight figure of the woman. After trying all fall semester to reduce his new intern to a quivering heap, and failing, campus gossip suggested Thelma might just beat the old buzzard at his own game. She'd managed to pull off every one of his unreasonable demands, if only by seconds, that he'd so far levied.

Thelma slapped the quiz master on the platen and grinned over her shoulder. "I'm getting to the picky bastard. He's softening. Last time he only gave me six minutes."

With a grimace Rose shoved her hand under a textbook and wiggled her fingers underneath a paperback about a mad Englishman, and retrieved the banana. She'd forgotten to eat it before class, the first time she'd remembered it was in there, too busy texting on her cell phone with her friend María.

"You might be wearing him down," she said in response to Thelma's claim, peeling back a strip of rubbery yellow skin.

Thelma's white teeth flashed as she expertly snatched the copies in batches and bounced them on the top of the copy machine, smoothing them into a neat pile.

"I'm going to get Edgestein to sponsor me."

Rose snorted a sound of disbelief at Thelma's claim. "I'd love to see you get hired as a real research associate, but he's never done it in the whole time he's been on staff."

Thelma looked sideways at her. "Never?" She waited until Rose confirmed the answer with a nod. "I'll be the first."

Rose stuffed a hunk of banana in her mouth and gave her thumbs up.

She inspected the fabric seams. The stitches showed strain, the threads pulling apart at the strap. Even if she didn't count the pad of paper, the scattering of pens and markers, the plastic-sleeved grade book, the trio of plastic jewel cases containing the CDs she still needed to find time to preview before showing in class, her personal items, and the debris of her breakfast, she was going to need to find a new method for transporting work materials. Her old bag had outlived its lifespan. She should probably try to look a bit more professional anyhow.

"Two minutes and counting." Thelma quipped and scooted out the door.

Rose listened to her retreating footsteps, mentally tracing Thelma's path as she sped down the polished asphalt tiles of the hall. The familiar squeal of the stairwell door indicated she'd opted for the quickest descent.

She broke off another chunk of banana and stuffed it in her mouth while she finished sorting mail. She dropped the announcements for video resources directly in the recycle bin, since the department had no money for purchasing instructional materials and her personal budget was zip. She read an announcement for a free textbook on a subject she didn't currently teach, but desk copies being a sweet perk, she saved the postcard. The faculty newsletter didn't even get a glance before being added to the blue plastic tub that served as a recycle bin. As a first-year adjunct faculty at the very bottom of the academic food chain, she couldn't even entertain opinions about the collective bargaining process without feeling foolish. The final sheet of paper at the bottom of the stack made her stop in mid-bite.

Employment announcement was emblazoned across the page header, just below the University letterhead emblem. Rose's gaze immediately locked on the words "Anthropology Department". The job announcement indicated the job she currently held was being offered as a contractual position.

She'd heard two tenured faculty members planned to go on sabbatical. Supposedly, the department was considering offering the classes to part-timers for the one-year duration of the leave. That meant the chance to have a full course load, and be paid a comparable salary, without having to earn tenure. Sure, it was only a ten months contract but the opportunity would do wonders to round out her vitae. Always a good attribute for future job hunting. She might also have the opportunity to teach additional courses, another chance to help fluff out her professional experiences.

Attention drawn back to the paper in her hand, Rose angled the page to wash dim natural light over the text, reducing the yellowed glare of the fluorescent tube lights in the room. She no longer heard the rain pattering against the wire-infused safety glass. In fact, her hearing had gone as numb and ineffectual as her brain while she read the title of the job position over and over until finally the words permeated her brain. Synapses connected and she envisioned the next academic year, herself vested importantly in the department.

A quick scan of the contents confirmed her suspicion. Tenured faculty split their academic load between teaching and research. Most taught four classes a year, two each semester and spent the rest of their contractual obligation conducting research. Adjunct faculty like her usually got assigned one or two classes if overloads were scheduled. With two additional full-time equivalent teaching loads opening up between four and six classes each semester, she might get to teach as many as three or four class preps. It would be a heavy load but such a great opportunity.

She tossed the peel in the trash and read the announcement in full. There weren't a lot of details. The basic list of requirements, which she met, was typical for teaching at this educational level. A general timeline for submitting application materials was typed at the bottom. No information about a date for formal interviews was listed. She wondered if she'd be required to conduct a teaching demonstration. At least she had enough classroom experience now to not make a complete fool of herself.

Rain slashed at the single small window above the copy machine. She noted the sky was grey and blotchy with dark clouds. The storm sliding down from the mountains brought freezing waves of rain. Not that they'd get any snow. She'd heard rumors of snow from people who'd lived in Sacramento their entire lives but the stories had the ring of myth and legend. This February however, was shaping up to be the wettest winter month in eight decades of central valley climatic history.

Rose knew she was popular with students. She had experienced no problems with staff or administration that would count as a black mark next to her name when the hiring committee was selected. Despite those facts, she might well find herself unemployed at the end of this semester unless she could prove she was the best candidate for the position. Teaching jobs were highly competitive. Every year produced a new batch of potential candidates, guaranteeing more applicants to select from than positions to be filled. Already, she had beaten a lot of other hopefuls for this academic cycle.

She had to keep her teaching position. Not only did she need the money to cover her living expenses while she finished her dissertation, she wanted to stay at Riverbend University. Her research focus was nearby and she didn't want to start over again, not personally or professionally. She'd stomp on the competition and establish herself as the perfect match for the department.

Then she'd interview and get the job.

No problem.

CHAPTER TWO

The Plan

Rose waited on the fourth floor as the elevator crept up from the basement level at the speed she imagined ancient trilobites had scuttled along the floor of some long-dead ocean. It was possible the mechanical device was even slower, but she never voiced the thought aloud since nobody outside the building would probably get her analogy, except maybe some of the folks over in biology. Some of them knew about Cambrian life forms. She leaned close to the crack in the door and heard the pulleys creaking as the old chain-driven mechanism heaved the shuddering passenger compartment skyward. The oldest buildings on campus dated back to the 1920s and the Social Science complex where she worked had been built in the 1950s. Nobody knew why the elevator looked and acted a hundred years old. The square box hoisted up and down the four floors of the building but always returned to the basement level when the last rider departed and no one pushed the keypad. Since the labs and personnel offices occupied the lowest level, affectionately called the dungeon by faculty and students alike, this fact was generally very convenient at the end of the day when she was ready to go home.

The rest of the time it was hurry-up-and-wait mode.

Like right now.

Rose leaned against the wall and waited. She was tired. The hall was relatively empty, the between-class traffic patterns slowing as the afternoon lengthened. It felt good to slump over and relax. After teaching both of her class sections today, she'd also covered Dr. Wilcox's advanced seminar class. The intensity had sapped the remainder of her energy. The upper-division level students were far more critical and argumentative, prepared to defend their position at all expense. Today's session had ended with a heated discussion between two groups of students bearing divergent but equally valid points of view. Mediating was worthwhile but it was also emotionally draining. The class was large, almost twice as many students scrambling for a seat at the start of the hour. Compared to when she'd enrolled for her undergraduate coursework, that was a big leap in numbers in a short timeframe.

Campus was crowded. The start of a new semester meant there were plenty of extra people still figuring out if they were going to stay or go. Dropout rates had fallen and increasingly tight budgets didn't extend far enough. Sluggish economic factors brought new droves of students to the university. Faculty felt obligated to overload their classes in an effort to accommodate the population growth. She personally found it difficult to turn down students desperate to enroll in any class, just to earn enough units to qualify for earlier registration dates for the next semester.

"Hey, Miss Brashear."

Rose looked up to see a perky blonde girl barreling down the hall. Mandy Essex was an intense and friendly young woman, who would someday be a brilliant politician with her broad perfect teeth and manicured mane. Rose smiled back a little crookedly. She liked Mandy well enough but the girl's mediocre student skills thus far had not endeared her as a favorite student.

"What are you teaching during the next summer session?" Mandy's smile was aimed like a tractor beam in one of those political rallies advertised on television.

Rose shook her head.

Although summer was still months away, the college had already made the decision to cut back summer course offerings. Tenured faculty had already claimed all available classes, leaving adjunct faculty facing unemployment.

Mandy's smile faltered. "Nothing? I really want to take another one of your classes."

The statement was flattering but Rose suspected it was because junior faculty like herself hadn't become hardened to the excuses and delaying tactics the more seasoned instructors no longer tolerated. Mandy was notoriously incompetent about submitting work on time. In her second year of teaching, Rose had yet to be disillusioned by the machinations of the student body. Besides, it still felt weird to be on the other side of the classroom. All those faces looking at her like she knew what she was talking about, sometimes made her feel like a fraud. Never mind that she was actually quite knowledgeable about anthropology, and her specializations within the field made her an expert in a narrow slice of the discipline. At times, the few years separating their ages felt like a mighty gap.

Mandy shivered all over, like one of those puppies in the Hallmark commercials around the holidays. "What about next fall?"

Rose shoved aside images of golden retrievers and shrugged. "The academic schedule for next year hasn't been finalized yet. If I find out anything before the end of session, I'll make an announcement about future course offerings."

The elevator door creaked open, the steel panel shuddering in the track. Rose stepped inside, blocking the access as Mandy delivered her speech a second time, her impassioned tone echoing oddly as the panel closed. The door shut and ended the conversation but brought home the realization that Rose had no fall-back plan for her future.

She was halfway through her advanced degree. The one year of coursework was completed. Some of her research was documented, the rest waiting to be summarized and compared. Then there was the dissertation to be written, and the subsequent oral defense to endure. She really needed the next year of teaching to finish. Being forced to find a job outside the academic arena meant she'd be at the mercy of someone else's schedule and possibly be unable to complete her surveys. A slow-down could hurt her future. If she was forced to go deeper into educational debt by taking out more loans, she'd spend the rest of her life paying them off. Even the low-interest loans could take decades to repay on a professor's salary, and since education was still the number one employer of anthropologists in the United States, the idea of going tens of thousands of dollars further in debt seemed extra foolish.

She needed to keep *this* job. Without another year of teaching under her belt and the completion of her degree, she'd be stuck behind a new wave of graduating professionals. Accolades and research were great, but in academia you rode the cresting wave or found yourself awash in the shallows. She'd rather that, than find herself treading water in the shark-infested deep but neither appealed. Rose had a plan, she always had a plan, but this one wasn't working out the way she'd envisioned.

First she needed to figure out what the anthropology department wanted in a new hire. Second was making sure she fit the details as tightly as possible. Third was making certain she outshone all the other potential candidates.

The elevator car finally creaked down to the basement level. Rose spilled out into the glare of fluorescent lighting. The hallway was empty. She headed to the nearest end, rounding the corner to spy the door to Dr. Wilcox's office standing open. It usually was, the door propped open with the taxidermied foot of an elephant.

Dr. Wilcox heard her come through the doorway. "Relax Rose. Nothing is going to happen until fall semester."

"But the job listing says the position begins next fall." She didn't try to curb the slight whine in her tone. The Doc was accustomed to her complaints.

"I can personally guarantee that come the end of August, you'll be scheduled for two classes, just like usual." He grinned at her. "Even after the review committee makes a final decision about a candidate, the new hire may not start until the following academic year. Everything is contingent on funding."

Some of the tension in her chest relaxed. This was welcome news. The one-year reprieve was enough time for her to finish up. Most, if not all, of her remaining research could be completed this summer. If she saved up enough income to spend the summer writing, she could finish early. Then if the worst happened and she didn't get the job, she could be reasonably assured of having a chance elsewhere.

Dr. Wilcox was looking at her with an expectant air.

"What?" she asked.

He waved both hands in the general direction of his desk. The entire surface was heaped with papers, stacks of them slumped over and spilling into other piles. "Do you know what I did with the card for Beverly's birthday?"

"Second stack from the left, beneath the blue folder which contains the edited version of the article you're supposed to submit to Archaeology Quarterly by the end of the month." Rose dropped everything on her desk and watched Dr. Wilcox pounce on the folder.

He extracted the yellow envelope from beneath and reached for his suitcoat. "I'm taking Beverly to dinner at Armallandi's Trattoria. Would you like me to bring you back the usual?"

Mouth salivating, Rose nodded. "Give my love to Beverly. I sent her an e-card." The full color photo had featured a dozen muscled men wearing kilts. Beverly had already written back expressing her appreciation.

Despite the negative ramifications to her professional career and the potential setback to her academic plans, the thing that most motivated Rose was the possibility of having to move home. She loved her parents but she didn't want to live with them. There were other options to consider, like moving somewhere else, or getting a roommate to cut down on her living expenses. She could and should apply for other jobs. A goose might drop a golden egg in her lap. Her research was here in the west and it was only smart to stay on this side of the country. Her recently granted access to the ranchlands of the García family in Nevada offered untapped historical, archaeological, and mining resources. Dr. Wilcox had greased the wheels for her future by providing input and access to his own colleagues. She'd taken advantage of that, like any good graduate assistant, but she had also proven her own abilities. Maybe she needed to see this challenge as a dual opportunity to prove herself worthy of the position, and avail herself of other teaching opportunities.

After Dr. Wilcox departed she settled down at her desk and opened a file on her computer. She titled it: Job Acquisition Plan.

CHAPTER THREE

The Competition

The next morning Rose arrived on campus, having worked late and slept badly. Fatigue was her excuse for avoiding the stairs today, especially since both of her classes were on the fourth floor. She saved her exercise for the field. Walking miles of rock-strewn dirt in scrub country while she studied the surface of the ground for cultural material kept her in decent shape.

Jonathon DeVries rounded the corner, coming from the opposite end of the hall. His face lit up when he saw her and he stretched his considerable stride, obviously intent on talking.

Rose stopped and waited for him.

He was tall and lanky. His height was accentuated by the black suit, pristine white shirt, and narrow pencil tie. In appearance he looked more like an FBI agent than a college professor. Despite the recent fashion trend in narrow neckties for men and squared off suit coats, it wasn't a style affectation. Jonathon was a fashion throwback to an earlier time. He could have fit into the McCarthy era without batting an eye, at least appearance-wise. Politically, she was pretty certain he wasn't a Communist.

Jonathon preferred black and white. He liked the contrast of positive and negative. Life in Jonathon's world never ranged into the outer layers found in old sepia-toned or gray-scale photographs. Unlike Rose's multigrained spectrum of qualifiers, Jonathon graded and assessed his students with an iron ruling akin to the Kaiser of Wilhelm back in the 1940s. He followed the rule of take-no-prisoners, pass-no-slackers, and no-task-is-too-small to require intensive effort.

Students adored him.

He and Rose became friends during freshmen year. Enrolled in a mandatory economic anthropology course, a nightmare class combining statistical analysis and socio-cultural interpretation, they combined mental powers and discovered they worked well as a team. The problem was they lacked similar academic interests. He liked tissue. She preferred bones.

"Did you see the announcement?" he asked when he was within reasonable speaking distance.

Rose nodded. The lack of preamble was typical. She had considered other potential candidates and eyed him with a jaundiced expression. Jonathon would be stiff competition, the worst kind, actually. He was smart and driven, and skilled.

He stopped beside her just as the elevator arrived. "You'll be applying, naturally."

A knot twisted in her stomach. "Of course. And you?" Of course he would. Being in the same state of employment limbo, he'd be crazy to pass up applying for any position that offered better income and a chance of permanency.

Jonathon's dark gaze met hers and slid sideways before he nodded. His mouth compressed in a flat line. "The state cut funding to all non-essential positions and the job offer I had from the California FBI crime lab fell through."

Rose sucked in a breath. This was a mighty blow. Jonathon had been excited about the potential job offer. He'd already been assured of the position but until the official word came through the pipeline, he wouldn't receive an offer. Now it wouldn't happen.

"That sucks. I'm sorry." She meant it. Even though she didn't want to compete against Jonathon's expertise in the job arena, he was still her friend. She knew this was a major blow.

They stepped inside the elevator and the car shuddered into motion.

Rose studied his face, caught a trace of lingering disappointment. He'd really wanted the position with the crime lab. "Is there any chance the job will be reopened or is the decision final?"

His shoulders slumped briefly as he sighed. "It's final for this fiscal year. I don't want to wait another twelve months for them to pull the same stunt. I passed up that position with the county investigative agency in order to wait for this and now I've got nothing."

She winced. She'd forgotten he'd actually turned down that offer. "If it makes you feel any better, I heard they disbanded the special task force that funded the county investigative team." She frowned because she wasn't certain what she had read in the paper was the same place that had tried to recruit him.

"That's beside the point." He said and huffed out a grumbling noise.

Rose rolled her eyes.

With an abrupt change of tenor, Jonathon whistled as the elevator door opened at the second floor and stepped off, turning around to look back at her. "Appreciate the support, Rose. Look, I know we're both good candidates and we both really want some job security. Despite the fact we'll be competing for the position, I think you should definitely apply."

She could see he understood the complications this might introduce into their friendship. "May the better applicant win, which is me, of course."

He smirked back at her.

For the moment she shied away from focusing on the employment announcement and studied him. Her arms were loaded with work-related materials; the beat-up bag strapped across her chest carried only her personal possessions today. "Why do you never have anything to carry?" she complained.

He moved his gaze up and down her body, taking in her mismatched slacks and jacket, clearly finding her bohemian appearance lacking. Looking smugly down at her, and emphasizing the foot difference in their heights, he spoke just as the door began to close. "Natty look, even for you, Rose."

She waited until after the elevator had started to climb again before venting her frustration.

Shit. Shit. Shit.

Things just got more complicated.

Jonathon had been her best guy friend since forever, all the way back to when they were brand-new wet-behind-the-ears, living-away-from-home-for-the-first-time, eighteen-year-old coeds. They'd been study-partners, all-night exam cram leaders at the student union, written student funding grant requests together, and even commiserated bad romances over pitchers of beer at the local pizza place. They'd never hooked up. An occasional rumor might drift through the department, suggesting they were a couple, and it never failed to produce amusement. When things got dull, Dr. Wilcox had been known to start new gossip just to sit back and watch the fallout.

Chemistry fizzled between Rose and Jonathon like a dud firecracker. She preferred romance that sizzled. Jonathon liked explosive relationships. They found love with other people but over the years had become good friends, maybe even best friends.

Through almost eighteen months of part-time teaching, they'd continued to collaborate and support each other in their classroom efforts. Jonathon was her friend, yes, but he was also a colleague and that required competitive respect. Only one person would be hired and that meant a dynamic shift in employment status. Adjunct faculty found solidarity in numbers. Once you moved up the salary ladder into a more permanent employment setting, you found yourself in a solitary role. Rose was sure their professional relationship would survive this challenge, but their personal one might well be fractured.

Jonathon had driven across town after midnight more than once when she'd found herself dumped by the heart throb of the month. She'd been his cheerleader too, especially after his girlfriend abandoned him to run off and conduct fieldwork in Turkey.

Elise had waltzed out the door without a backward glance. Jonathon had been devastated. He hadn't been on the verge of proposing but he'd definitely been hunkered down and ready to do the long-term girlfriend routine. Rose could still picture the scene in her mind. The couple would date until the FBI or some other important agency offered him the Fox Mulderish job of his dreams, then he'd suggest they move in together. Before you could count to five, there would be a house with a Buick parked in the drive, a white picket fence to fence in the collie, and the requisite two kids. The problem was Elise had not been that kind of girl. She was more like the witch who escaped the Salem trials because she was too busy accusing innocent young girls of duplicity.

She had not been Elise's bosom buddy.

Rose had patched up Jonathon's injured self-esteem as best she could and had take-out delivered to his apartment so many times, she had to resume jogging to keep the seams of her jeans from splitting. He, on the other hand, had never gained an ounce.

Finally he had ventured back into the mainstream. They had buried his sorrows with one final night of slamming cinnamon schnapps in the lab afterhours and inventorying the taxonomic collection.

After three shots he had admitted his relationship with Elise had been more physical than emotional.

A few drinks later Rose had admitted she didn't blame Elise for ditching him in favor of Çatalhöyük. In her opinion no man measured up beside access to a world-class Neolithic site. Rose had told him she would have dumped his ass too.

By then Jonathon was drunk enough he agreed.

There was nothing she could do about the current situation. They were both going to apply for the position and they would simply have to make the best of it. They'd already weathered plenty of ups and downs, surely they could make it through this too. Rose hoped so. She had few enough friends in her life, especially now that she'd sworn off dating.

CHAPTER FOUR

The Vitae

Rose stepped out of the elevator and into the arms of Dr. Crenshaw. He embraced her with a fervor that produced an appreciative grin. At least one man on earth wanted to hold her tight against his chest. Although he brightened her mood, and she adored Dr. Crenshaw, the emeritus professor of paleontology was the last person she wanted to see today. A lovely old man with the emphasis on prehistoric, he had the skills of 007 when it came to ferreting out information and the charm. She suspected he'd been lurking about, waiting for her to appear, in order to assess reaction to the job announcement. Officially Jonathon's mentor, he was fond of her, mostly because she flirted back with him, a harmless activity with only an occasionally alarming result. Capable of stretching a brief exchange of pleasantries into an hour-long investigation of one's private affairs, he wasted no time with preamble.

"Good afternoon, Miss Brashear. I am delighted to be in your presence once again." He bent down and placed a gentle kiss on her cheek. He beamed at her stutter and slipped a tailored arm through hers, falling into step beside her. "Dare I hope you intend to apply for the departmental position next fall?"

She murmured the appropriate yes response. Dr. Crenshaw topped her by at least six inches but being slightly bowed from age and having a gracile build made them more equal in scale. Rose tried to keep her admiration secret since he responded to any encouragement with enthusiasm. He smelled like peppermints and if he'd been forty years younger she wouldn't have resisted his Old World charm. Okay, even thirty years younger, but she had to draw a limit somewhere. As it was, he proved adept at stealing kisses beneath strategically located mistletoe bundles. He'd taken her by surprise at a holiday party last December, a memory that still left her with a weird mix of appreciation and ick factor.

She'd enrolled in undergraduate paleontology with Dr. Crenshaw and learned loads of fascinating information, most of it useless for practical daily living. Though he specialized in forensics now, he'd begun his career in Devonian evolutionary science. He'd been a fixture in the academic community for so many decades that people forgot he had excavated bony fish fossils in Mongolia back before the borders closed to outsiders. Independently wealthy and knowing dignitaries from all over the globe by their first names, he crossed social boundaries and bridged generations with ease. An invitation to Dr. Crenshaw's annual Christmas bash scored the bearer considerable bragging rights, and the possibility of hobnobbing with genuine movers and shakers.

Her first semester on campus he'd asked Rose if she was related to Archimedes Bannion, an adventurer of some disrepute from his own generation. He'd noted her middle name on the enrollment list and made the connection. Delighted when she'd confirmed Mede Bannion had been her grandfather, he'd treated her to coffee at the faculty dining hall so they could swap stories.

No one knew how many languages Dr. Crenshaw spoke fluently, but at last count Jonathon had confirmed seven. She willingly believed pretty much anything about the old guy. Certain she'd heard him spout a stream of Arabic once, although she'd been tipsy at the time and might have imagined the entire thing, Jonathon had dismissed her claim as invalid without independent confirmation. Spoilsport.

"I have an appointment with young Mr. DeVries this afternoon, just a fill-in-the-voids meeting about his dissertation project."

Speak of the devil.

Rose didn't bother replying. There was no need. Dr. Crenshaw would continue his stream of conversation, unabated until she left him standing outside the door of her classroom. Then he'd attach himself to the nearest faculty member who crossed his path until he'd worked his way up and down the hallway of each floor. Afterwards he'd go home and write a book or publish an article and win another award. He did things like that.

"So, my dear, what do you think about that idea?"

Caught not paying attention, Rose smiled at him. "Your ideas are always brilliant."

"Ah, then shall I expect one of you will have murdered the other before the hiring committee makes a decision?"

Rose flushed.

He laughed gently. "You flatter an old man and I tease you unmercifully." Patting her hand he leaned against her shoulder and dropped his voice in tone. "You were the only student who ever gave Jonathon real competition in my class and yet, you became friends. Mind a word of advice from someone who has walked these halls too many decades, don't let any job steal away the people who matter to you."

On impulse she leaned over and kissed his cheek. "Thanks, Dr. Crenshaw. If you were twenty years younger... I'm just saying."

He laughed at her and winked. With a flourish he released her arm, depositing her before the door to her classroom. She slipped inside, a flutter of emotion warming her cheeks. Playing both sides, the clever old devil had probably given Jonathon the same pep talk.

Rose wondered when new information would be posted regarding the job. She was anxious to learn when interviews would be scheduled, but all she'd been able to pry from anyone was an indeterminate date sometime before the end of spring session. She found it more difficult to concentrate on teaching and grading with her mind distracted by thoughts of how she could improve her hiring potential.

The hours of the afternoon ran together, becoming a precursor of the remainder of the week. It wasn't until Friday that she ran into Jonathon again, in the faculty mailroom. His always pale complexion, the product of rarely venturing outside during the sunlight hours, appeared even more washed out than usual.

"Have you slept this week?" She checked his clothes but they looked as immaculate as ever.

"It's my vampiric look. They're all the rage right now, popular with the in-crowd, you know." He sifted through the stack of flyers and envelopes from his box, dumping most of them into the recycling bin.

"Your vibe is more cadaverous than vampiric, although zombies are the hot ticket item this season, so I guess you're still trendy. Ghoulish is in." She flicked an imaginary dust mote off his suit coat.

Jonathon yawned. "I've been filling out paperwork every night, applying for various things." He didn't elaborate.

The evasion was warranted. She had no idea if he was seeking grants to outfit the lab with equipment the college wouldn't provide or searching out internships designed to increase his odds of getting the job. Rose pursed her lips. She hadn't gotten that far yet, and if Jonathon had, then she was behind schedule.

Jonathon left for class.

Rose had made an excuse to avoid their standing movie night the previous Wednesday. She hated to give up their regular theater visit but spending an evening of work-time out in the company of the competition seemed wasteful.

They parted amicably.

Rose spent the entire weekend updating and refining her vitae. When she received a text from Jonathon, nixing their usual lunchtime sprawl in Dr. Wilcox's office, she felt a twinge of regret mixed with relief. She could appreciate the act was half in retaliation to her ditching movie night, but figured he was struggling with the awkwardness of the situation too. At least the alone-time allowed her plenty more opportunity to sulk and plot.

Lonelier than she'd been in a long time, Rose realized how singular her personal life had become. Without Jonathon as a distraction, she graded papers and developed curriculum between classes. As a result, she ran out of things to do in the evenings. Busier than she could ever remember being, her life was emptier too.

Rose needed more friends. Maybe she should date once in a while, say yes the next time she got asked out. The trouble with that idea was her lack of desire to do the mating dance thing: it required too much work. After a series of lackluster dates, she'd given up on finding companionship for a while. If a guy couldn't entice her to go out for a latte or take a walk in the park, she didn't even think about making dinner plans. She'd read that exercise was supposed to produce a surge of endorphins, much like sex. Going out for a run was less complicated but also less enticing. Instead, she called her friend María and poured out her woes over the phone.

"I wish I had time to drive through the mountains for a quick visit," Rose said.

"Room four is yours for the asking, Rosie. Personally, I think you need to find a hot man and have a torrid affair, but that's just me."

Rose made a rude sound. "Yeah, 'cause that's worked so well for me in the past."

"Suck it up, chica. You know what they say, 'there's someone for everyone' and if that's a lie then we're both screwed. You could always ditch class for a week and come here. Nevada waits for everyone."

The idea of escaping to the chaparral for a few days was tantalizing.

Rose loved having dedicated private space in her friend's small motel. She'd spent a lot of time in the tiny town over the last couple of years, burning up miles of interstate while she drove back and forth every day during her fieldwork excursions. The locale was a short distance beyond the city of

Reno and only a few hours' drive through the mountains from Sacramento.

"You have no idea how tempting that sounds, María. Maybe over spring break? By April I'll be batshit bonkers and desperate to escape."

"Drink some wine and stay away from the nightclubs, you make poor decisions when you've been drinking. In the meantime I'll call Roberto and remind him to send a ranch hand out to check the security on the mine entrance."

"Glad I can provide a reasonably valid excuse to help move your love life to the next level. Any progress happening there?" María's would-be romantic interest was proving difficult to land.

"Not yet but hope springs eternal, right? I got to go Rose, a customer just pulled in." María made kissing noises and disconnected.

For a moment Rose contemplated packing a bag and driving to the tiny motel but rejected the impulse. She got off the couch and made a cup of coffee, poured in a nice dollop of cream, and dove back into her vitae.

CHAPTER FIVE

The Strategy

Rose slumped in her desk chair. All the air had been sucked out of her lungs. "What do you mean, you've been recused?"

Across the room, Dr. Wilcox's weathered face wrinkled into a topographic map of crisscrossing lines. Long years of field exposure had aged him prematurely.

"It means, my dear girl, I shall not sit on the hiring committee for the new position." He grinned at her dismay and waggled a crooked index finger. "Everybody knows I wouldn't be fair in assessing the other candidates. If I even thought of considering anyone but you, Beverly would make me suffer. For the sake of continued marital bliss I asked to be excused."

Rose flung herself across her desk in a dramatic display. "I'll never get the job now."

He laughed at her wail.

She wanted to deny his words but recognized a kernel of truth in his claim. If she got the position, Dr. Wilcox's presence on the committee would have left her wondering whether favoritism had played a role in her success.

"You've already earned my vote of confidence, Rose. You're an excellent candidate. I realize this advice doesn't help right now, but you don't want to be selected for any position for which you aren't a perfect match."

Rose still felt as if she'd lost a tiny margin of lead. Her confidence crumbled like five-day old cookies.

The Doc and his wife had been staunch supporters of her academic efforts, but nobody ever claimed Rose hadn't worked her backside off. Beverly pointed out how much her husband required a keeper and after taking responsibility for managing the domestic side, determined a like need to monitor the professional. Rose had been appointed. The arrangement proved symbiotic. Rose was a natural organizer and Dr. Wilcox didn't comprehend the concept.

"So much for manipulating the old boy network," Rose muttered, her cheek pressed against the scarred surface of her vintage walnut desk.

A snort of laughter rumbled out of Dr. Wilcox. "You need to be male and elderly."

"I had you. I thought," Rose countered. She lifted her head and jerked her chin toward his desk. "Don't forget to sign the change-of-grade form for Adelaide. She's coming by to pick it up tomorrow."

She pushed up into a sitting position and began straightening the stack of journals he'd dumped on the corner of her desk. Movement was better than sedentary pouting. Moving and sulking pacified her need to expel energy and still let her fuss about this disappointment. She wondered why the Doc had hauled out dozens of back issues of the *Journal of Historic Archaeology* but was too grumpy to ask. She stacked the journals into two piles at the edge of the bookcase shelf where current projects had been dumped. If she hadn't cleared off a space earlier in the morning nothing more would have fit.

The constant state of disarray in the office was countered only by her continual efforts to organize, process, clean and file. She worked her way across her desk to the nearest bookcase while Dr. Wilcox belabored the point.

"Cheer up. It's not such a huge setback. You're still the best candidate, even if Jonathon applies. He's a brilliant young man but he's more interested in biological concerns. The anthropology department needs someone who has a firm handle on historical preservation and osteological materials. Your research demonstrates strengths in both, and you have background in cultural matters, as well as the fossil record."

He swiveled his chair and yanked a massive binder off a teetering pile. He flopped the white spine over a stack of periodicals in the center of his desk and stabbed the interior with an index finger.

He pinned Rose with an intense stare. "This is what we need."

She crossed the six square feet of open space to look at his finding.

Dr. Wilcox's digit was centered on a photograph. The picture displayed a collection of hundreds of skeletal elements, several specimens laid out in proper taxonomic order on the top of tables. She recognized the deer skeleton even though the bones were like one of those exploded diagrams of electronic devices, the kind where all the components are separated and labeled. In fact, that was pretty much the reason for taxonomic samples. They provided schematics for matching up comparisons. She leaned down to look closer at the picture. Boxes and containers sat stacked in narrow towers, making a miniature city skyline of skyscrapers, except these were filled with the skeletons of animals.

A light sparked in the back of her mind, like the flare of sulfurous burst in an old blue tipped wooden match.

The picture didn't show details but Rose saw enough to identify the familiar domesticates common to most historical sites. She often compared isolated bone fragments and skeletal elements recovered from recent archaeological deposits with known and identified samples. She'd learned through trial and error how certain bones, especially those that were more common, could serve as important indicators. In her experience most of the faunal remains encountered in archaeological contexts resulted from food acquisition practices. The men who had worked the mining sites she explored, had consumed a fair amount of meat, primarily sourced from beef cattle. Since her research focused on nineteenth century mineralogical industry, in order to be certain of the identification, she'd amassed a collection of specimens. Rather than complete skeletons, she'd collected the commonly found parts.

Her focus intensified. She pulled the binder from underneath Dr. Wilcox's hand and spun it around, hunching over to peer at the background in the photo.

Taxonomic specimens were expensive, so costly that most colleges rejected the idea of spending money on the acquisition of samples. Orders were nixed with the excuse that they would benefit too few faculty. Denied. No budgetary allocation permitted. Departmental emphasis in recent years had focused exclusively on expanding the documentary film collection.

Rose straightened and closed her eyes to think. Collecting taxonomic specimens presented a set of challenges. A tingle of awareness shivered up her spine. If she acquired enough samples to broaden the department's meager coffers, her efforts would be seen as a positive attribute by most of the committee members. Granted, skeletal material didn't appeal to everyone, but even as much as Rose abhorred working with tissue, she'd macerate anything short of a human being to solidify her position in the number one slot on the queue. A larger and more comprehensive collection of bones benefited multiple courses taught in the division. By default, at least a few faculty members would appreciate her gesture.

Hell yes!

She'd jump into the roadkill business with enthusiasm. Wet work was all in a day's normal activity for Jonathon. Too bad the weirdo now counted as competition. She could use some help moving the larger animals.

Rose cheered up. Things might be worse.

Dr. Wilcox not being on the actual hiring committee was a disappointment, but that meant he wouldn't have to play nice. All the gossip and innuendo filtering down the pike as the months progressed would be shared, a fact which might prove beneficial in helping to establish the best approach to interviewing for the position. She just had to listen and refine her plans.

"Oh, and there's one more thing you should know, Rose."

The Doc cleared his throat and her stomach plummeted. Rose knew the signs. He only did the throat-clearing hack when he was on the verge of delivering news likely to be received in a bad way.

She raised her gaze from the photograph and met his watery blue eyes. She hitched her brows in an arc of inquiry and waited.

"Dr. Snodgrass will be taking my place."

Rose didn't even try to hide the grimace of distaste this news provoked. "That just sucks."

Dr. Wilcox murmured his agreement.

She paced across the confined space. "Her specialty is prehistory. She dismisses historical archaeology as a waste of good resources." Rose stopped and glanced back at the picture on Dr. Wilcox's desk. "Oh, you smooth devil. This is the one thing Snoddy would kill to have at her disposal. If I can collect enough wildlife samples to match the faunal remains found in prehistoric sites, then even the disagreeable Dr. Snodgrass might support my hire."

Dr. Wilcox's smile went wicked, offering a glimpse of the charm responsible for snagging his beauty queen wife. "That's the idea."

Rose steepled her fingers together and frowned. "I need to find lots of roadkill."

CHAPTER SIX

The Stakes

The stretch of hallway between her classroom door and the elevator began to feel like a narrow version of a Roman gladiator ring. Every time Rose went to or from class, she faced the gauntlet. Today's competition featured the lethal Dr. Snodgrass.

Among the least-liked professors on campus, and tied in the unpopularity contest with Dr. Edgestein, Snoddy was equally abhorred by introductory and advanced students alike. The woman's lousy reputation had been earned. She boasted the highest incidence of attrition in the entire department, failing as many undergrads as she passed. Back in the day, she'd climbed the academic ladder at a time when the old boy network was definitively misogynistic. The chip on her shoulder remained sharp enough to draw blood.

Rose supposed Snoddy had earned the hard edges on her personality, seeing how she'd been one of the women who broke through the glass ceiling and earned tenure in an academic position during an era when the classroom was dominated by male Professors. In many ways, women like Snoddy had forged new trails through the academic jungle, opening paths along the way for other women to follow. Like Rose.

Although eligible for retirement, campus gossip indicated Snoddy wouldn't go out without a fight. She showed no interest in going gentle into that good night. She'd ridden the wave of the feminism flag, landing a cushy tenure position straight out of college and charging into the field, full steam ahead. She manipulated family links to economic leaders in America and milked aristocratic connections in Europe. Everywhere she tread, Snoddy had embraced her reputation as a modern female and used her body as evolution had intended.

Rose believed the stories. She'd seen some of the vintage departmental photographs and almost admired the woman for her audacity. Dr. Snodgrass came from an old American family. The words Mayflower never fell from her lips, but no one ever forgot she was connected. Even without those accolades, she'd done well for herself. She'd been successful in the discipline, publishing regularly and contributing good scholarly rhetoric to academic journals on both sides of the Atlantic.

Despite her accomplishments, Rose couldn't appreciate the awful woman. She'd received more than one sharp remark in her undergraduate days and hadn't missed the fräulein one bit during the two year hiatus overseas when the woman had been a visiting scholar at an Italian institution. Snoddy had resumed regular teaching duties in Rose's last semester of coursework and she'd managed to avoid taking any more classes from the woman, a fact for which she was profoundly grateful now.

Dr. Snodgrass had polished her superiority play to perfection, halting in the hall and waiting for her prey to approach. Responding like the lowly serf she resembled, Rose approached the lady of the manor, moving right into the woman's hands. Her goal of reaching the stairwell or the elevator seemed impossible. Rose was almost within arm's reach before she recognized the second woman standing behind Snoddy's shoulder. Her step faltered. Like the proverbial bad penny, Elise Drummel had turned up again. Jonathon's ex-romantic entanglement was back from fieldwork in Turkey.

Rose recovered almost immediately and pasted a smile on her face, twisting her mouth into a semblance of a pleasant expression. She blurted out a greeting to both women.

Pleasantries exchanged in the time-honored tradition of equals meeting on the battlefield, served primarily for showmanship. Rose couldn't win a skirmish with a senior faculty member, at least not without opening herself to disciplinary action. Nevertheless, she prepared for battle, facing off against the older woman as streams of students passed them in the hallway, oblivious to the contest of wills about to take place.

"So glad to see you, Rose." Dr. Snodgrass motioned to Elise as if presenting a selection on a game show stage. "Elise is able to renew her teaching responsibilities on my behalf since I'll be taking Willy's place on the hiring committee."

Prepared for that juicy little tidbit at least, Rose nodded politely. She thought she detected a slight disappointment in Snoddy's narrow face. The woman must have been expecting to elicit greater shock and she enjoyed depriving her the satisfaction, petty though it was.

"Yes, indeed." Rose swiveled her attention to Elise and offered a greeting.

Elise stared back coldly, not meeting her eyes. "I don't want your competitive nature to disrupt our working relationship. I will also be applying for the position." She ignored the pleasantry altogether, her words clipped enough to chill white wine.

For a second Rose considered making a snarky comment. Something like since *she* intended to apply for the job, there'd be no competition, but instead she opted for the higher road. "I know our friendship is strong enough to withstand any strain."

Dr. Snodgrass didn't quite manage to cut off her snort of disbelief. The woman turned away, dismissing her.

Rose listened to her confirm a later appointment with Elise, and then watched her sashay down the hall.

The employment odds just shifted again. The position was exclusive to internal applicants and now they numbered at least three. Who knew how many others lurked in the halls? A number of doctoral candidates still kicked around campus, completing projects. Any one of them might prove to be a tough competitor. Rose and Jonathon weren't the only adjunct lecturers teaching in the department. The cultural anthropology focus could offer up at least one or two candidates. Everyone shared equal qualifications. At least that made for an open playing field. The trick would be to offer up a different kind of expertise that appealed to each faction of the department.

Elise turned back to face her, a crooked grin twisting her mouth, as if she were a bit pained by the effort involved.

"I didn't expect you to still be hanging around campus. Figured you'd be out grubbing in the dirt like Dr. Wilcox's good little minion."

Rose dismissed the idea. Following the nature of the crocodile she emulated, Elise never expressed sorrow or regret for any action undertaken.

"Minions have to stay close to their leader. It's a rule. I'm surprised you didn't know, considering your attachment to Snoddy." Rose adjusted the load of stuff in her hands and tried to figure out a way to escape without giving the impression she was fleeing.

Elise sneered a response in her direction.

It wasn't like the woman needed to be underhanded, she was brilliant and driven. Rose had seen the proof, firsthand. Elise had managed to damage Jonathon's ego, a not insubstantial organ in-and-of-itself. That was one hell of an achievement. The memory reminded Rose of the hours she'd put in massaging the bruised heart of the fallen hero.

Conflicting emotions warred inside for a moment.

Despite blaming Elise for Jonathon's heartache, Rose was honest enough to know that if someone offered her the choice between a bed buddy and a Neolithic site lusted after by every single person in prehistoric studies, well, she'd have been headed to the Middle East too.

Probably not a fair equation considering the idea of snuggling up to Jonathon's bony frame held zero appeal for her.

If rules didn't apply in love and battle, getting an academic position must constitute a serious skirmish. The flame between Jonathon and Elise might be reignited. While they busily rekindled their romance, Rose could piece together an impressive taxonomic sample to fortify her stance. Nevermind she'd wanted to punch Elise in the months after the woman had ditched Jonathon. That was the past, this was the present, and the job represented her future.

She leaned in close. "Have you seen Jonathon yet?"

Elise's face underwent a dramatic transformation. Her eyes widened even as her lips went flat in a compressed line. Her cheekbones stood out in stark ridges, framed by her impressive mane of curls. They had made an attractive couple.

Jonathon's sleek black hair was the perfect foil for Elise's white-blonde.

"I didn't expect you, of all people, to twist the knife, Rose. I'm glad to know how things are going to be. So much for trying to keep this civilized." And with that, she strode away.

Rose stood like a rock in a riverbed, the swirl of humanity flowing around her in currents. Impossible though it seemed, tears had shone in Elise's eyes.

CHAPTER SEVEN

The Bargain

Rose tilted up her beer bottle and swallowed deep. Even in the basement of the building, people came and went at random times so she'd made certain the door to the office was locked. She tapped the top of her desk with her beer bottle. "You should have told me that Elise thinks we're carrying on. The very idea is ridiculous. She never thought that when you and she were dating." She watched Jonathon roll his beer between his hands.

His features scrunched up. "I told you, there wasn't time. They ambushed me."

"You could have texted. I was in class for two and a half hours."

"Be reasonable Rose, what would I have said?" He made quote marks in the air next to his ears, his index finger wrapped around the neck of the beer bottle positioning it at an awkward angle. "Watch out. Elise is back and ready to brawl. I accidently made her think you and I are a hot ticket item."

Rose flipped him the finger. She knew she might be unreasonable but she wasn't willing to concede that yet. "Sure, why not? You could have said, 'Hey, Elise is back and has some screwed up ideas about you and me doing the slow polka'."

He raised one eyebrow and repeated her last three words, mouthing the phrase without uttering any sound.

A laugh burbled up. "Okay, I admit it was a matter of bad timing. I still feel like a bitch because Elise thinks I deliberately set out to twist the screws."

Jonathon said nothing.

Rose slanted a suspicious look at him. "Did she really proposition you to pick up where things left off almost two years ago?"

He nodded an affirmation.

"That's ballsy." She said after a moment.

His gaze stayed on the far wall.

She sensed that the flame might not be entirely extinguished. That was too bad, in her opinion, because it boded ill for Jonathon's future.

After Elise had skipped the country Jonathon had rebounded slowly. While the couple's relationship around campus had been viewed as a casual alliance, not a committed one-to-one sort of thing, nobody paid much attention at first. Elise made a practice of discarding men like last season's handbag. When Jonathon didn't snap out of his slump after a few weeks, Rose had dragged him to a bar for an interrogation. It worked. She'd badgered him with questions until he'd finally admitted his feelings had run deep.

"Love doesn't listen to the mind shouting about common sense" he said, tossing back a bourbon, straight up.

Rose still thought those words had held certain eloquence. She eyed him now, experiencing a momentary twinge of guilt. "I had every intention of throwing you under the bus."

He offered her an outraged look.

"Don't be dramatic. You'd do the same if it meant they'd offer you the job."

He toasted her with his bottle of beer.

She felt relief that the misunderstanding had placed an obstacle between the former lovers. Not that she didn't want Jonathon to be happy, but she had no desire to live through the demise of another aborted romance featuring Elise as the central star.

He tipped back in the chair, crossing his ankles and slouching like a teenager, while he drained the last of his beer.

She considered him with an objective eye. He wasn't a bad looking guy, if you liked them tall and brainy, in a sort of old school principal sort of way. Photographs of scientists from the Manhattan Project or the atomic testing blasts in Nevada always brought to mind images of Jonathon. The image reminded her of something he said one night as he dropped her off at home.   She'd just been dumped by her date, the quarterback of the campus football team had left the club with a woman he'd met on the dance floor, and she'd called Jonathon for a ride. He had not been impressed when his phone rang at midnight, but since Elise had left by then, he was sitting at home alone.

"Of course, I'll come get you. Why don't you date chemists or physicists? What is it with you and these muscled-over jocks?" he'd demanded.

Rose considered his question long after he'd dropped her off at home and driven away. She knew the answer stemmed from the familiar old insecurity. No matter what she accomplished or how much she achieved, there was that nagging sense of not being good enough. Coming from her family of extrovert over-achievers, she'd never felt like she measured up. She resolved to make a change. She gave up romancing athletes and took up field research.

She'd later confessed in an alcohol induced haze at the local pizza parlor, "what is the point of hooking up with a guy who simply calls the next number on his phone every time you aren't available for a tryst?"

Jonathon had agreed. "The men you date are pigs."

"You're so metrosexual."

He'd peered across the table at her, his eyes bleary. "I can't be insulted if I don't know what the hell you're talking about."

They'd staggered three blocks to his apartment and collapsed on the furniture. It was the start of a regular Wednesday night cycle. First they went to the movie theater and watched the new release. They never even bothered to check what was playing, they just showed up for the 6:30 viewing. The film was followed by a medium pizza, the all-meat toppings the only thing they agreed on, and at least one pitcher of beer. Sometimes two.

They skipped cocktails at the corner dive since Jonathon had an early anatomical dissection class the next morning. As he said, "The smell of decomposition is harder to take with a queasy stomach and a hangover."

Dates were reserved for other nights and other people. People assumed she and Jonathon were friends-with-benefits, but they were just friends. Now they were adversaries of a sort and it felt odd.

Rose pushed away the memories and turned her attention back to Jonathon.

"Did you just have a senior moment? I thought I was going to have to splash water on your face to wake you up." Jonathon was leaned forward in his seat.

She pointed at the water bottle in his hand. "Put that down. I was reminiscing. So, Elise thinks we're together because you said you preferred my company to hers."

He nodded and slouched back in his chair. "True, you know. I do prefer your company."

Rose toasted him with her bottle but she heard the tiny note of uncertainty in his voice.

"She's stiff competition." Rose emptied her beer and set the bottle on the corner of her desk. "Even if she didn't misinterpret what you said, it would still be difficult for you guys to split the sheets and apply for the same position."

Jonathon snaked another beer out of the small refrigerator on the shelf and offered it to her. She shook her head. She'd driven today and didn't want to risk another drink.

Twisting the cap off the bottle Jonathon pierced her with a glare. "How come Dr. Snodgrass isn't being recused from the committee? Elise has been her academic pet for years. If Dr. Wilcox had to be removed because of potential favoritism for you, what gives with Snoddy?"

"Elise has been out of the country long enough that I guess she's no longer linked to her mentor in the same way I am to mine." Rose exhaled and leaned back in her chair. A headache loomed behind her eye sockets. "Elise is a really strong candidate. Aside from our personal issues, she's good at what she does and she's got all that practical experience with artifacts from Çatalhöyük. I saw the online proofs of several pages of the catalog inventory. Her name is all over half the entries because she worked with the photographic specialist on site."

"The only saving grace is the book won't be published for another year." Jonathon nursed his beer. "We need to figure out what we can offer the department that Elise can't. The only thing I've been able to come up with is to expand the taxonomic collections."

Rose's wince produced a bark of laughter.

"I guess you thought of that too," Jonathon said.

Rose studied his face. He looked as tired as she felt. Mental fatigue rather than physical exhaustion caused by the fact they'd had too many emotional highs and lows lately.

She held up one hand and ticked points off her fingers. "Your specialization in forensic analysis overlaps the anthropology department with other fields. You pull medical and biology majors, criminal studies, and even students from the administration of justice program. Hiring you to teach on a permanent basis benefits a more diverse population than what I do."

Additionally, Jonathon's job involved some distasteful although fascinating, work. He knew bones as well as she did and he also knew how to process them. In fact they had rigged up a processing case in the corner of his lab and filled it with dermestid insects last year. Now they instructed students how to clean samples when someone stumbled across a dead squirrel.

He responded with his own list. "Your specialization in historic site evaluation has some practical application to the university. Not only can you teach classes, but you evaluate archaeological sites as a cultural resources management consultant, and you've worked with local law enforcement in identifying the age of human remains. That's a lot of good press for the university as well as our individual college programs."

He was right. It just sounded so much better when she heard it from someone else. The last time she had determined the historicity of a set of human remains discovered on a nearby farm. The skeleton had not been the murder victim police detectives had been hoping they'd finally located, but rather a nineteenth century historic burial, probably from an old settlement.

"Most of our colleagues find your work distasteful and my work boring. That leaves Elise in the spotlight with her exotic and impressive site locale history." Rose pinned Jonathon with her gaze. "So, here's my proposition: why don't we team up? We can compile a large enough collection of remains to impress the hell out of the committee. Between us we can offer not just domestic and wild taxons, but laboratory and even human materials. If we combine forces, haunt the highways, and pull in favors from people we know, we can divvy up the results before interview time."

Jonathon's smirk quickly turned to a grin. "I'm in." He straightened in his chair and leaned forward, stretching out a hand. "We can push Elise firmly out of the running but then it's a sprint to the finish line, every woman for herself."

Rose slapped her hand in his and shook. "Your legs may be longer, weirdo, but I've got more stamina."

"So, is this one of those times when we're supposed to keep our friends close and our enemies closer?" Jonathon's smile, still in place, showed a hint of strain.

Rose nodded. "From here on out, you're my best frenemy."

CHAPTER EIGHT

The Specimens

Rose yanked the neoprene glove over her palm and snapped the wristband. It was silent on the dark country road even though it wasn't that late. That was the great thing about living in Sacramento, it didn't take long to get out of the city proper, and the surrounding terrain offered lots of variation.

"What is up with the undergrads taking sides?" she asked.

Jonathon grunted as he maneuvered the hindquarters of the deer so it aligned with the bed of the truck. "You can thank Dr. Wilcox for that idea. Yeah, I figured it out when half my dissection students showed up with rose paraphernalia stuck in their hair or pinned to their shirts."

Picking up the forelegs, Rose struggled to lift her half of the doe high enough to slide the carcass onto the lowered tailgate. She puffed with the effort. "And, I have half the baseball team in my afternoon section and they're all wearing the letter J spelled out in electrical tape on their jerseys. Whose idea was that?"

A whoop of laughter was his only response.

She concentrated on holding the deer while Jonathon moved his grip and shoved the roadkill in far enough to shut the tailgate. At least this one was intact. The last one they'd found had been so mangled they'd passed on picking it up.

He latched the gate and stripped off his gloves, automatically rolling them together, inside out. "The captain of the baseball team passed my class last semester, but only because I let him take the final exam at a special time so he could make some playoff game. As a result, Team Jonathon grows by leaps and bounds."

Rose made a rude sound. "It's ridiculous. They don't care who teaches the class, just who gives them the best opportunity to pass."

Jonathon moved toward the driver's door. "That means they all hate Elise."

"There is that."

Elise might successfully woo the hiring committee but the students despised her teaching methods. Ever since she'd taken over Dr. Snodgrass's Introduction to Prehistory class, the attrition rate had climbed. Spring drop-out rates were high to begin with but scuttlebutt suggested students numbering in the double digits had fled the classroom.

Jonathon started the engine as she climbed in the passenger side, shifting into gear and pulling the vehicle away from the pick-up site before flipping on the headlights. He drove in silence for a while until they approached the street that led back to the campus perimeter road. "Exactly what are we going to do with a fully grown deer? There's no way to process it in the lab, she won't fit inside the dermestid tank."

"I rigged up a trough on the roof." Rose ignored his skeptical expression. She was fairly certain it would work – although if it didn't they were going to have an extremely smelly situation on their hands.

Rodrigo, the night custodian, had long ago accepted that the comings and goings of junior faculty were better left uninvestigated. He steadfastly turned a blind eye whenever he saw Jonathon's truck pull up at the rear loading dock. Even without the challenge of getting the deer into the elevator for the ride up to the top floor, and then maneuvered up the final flight of stairs to the roof, processing an animal the size of a deer was going to be stinky. Not for the first time Rose wondered if it would be better to find a remote stretch of road, wrap it in chicken wire, and let nature do the work. Except the likelihood of losing the smaller bones was greater, as was damage from rodents and carrion consumers.

No, this was the best choice. Jonathon knew it too. He hadn't argued nearly as vociferously about the deer as he had about the trio of skunks last week. They'd come out of the cleaning tank in excellent shape and a quick peroxide bath had prettied them up nicely. Vindication felt good.

If it hadn't been for the rumors circulating around campus for the last two weeks, Rose wouldn't have pressed for the deer, but Elise had gone and done something nastily underhanded. She'd suggested the fake romance between Rose and Jonathon was inappropriate. The college had no discernible policy regarding afterhours romancing. Lord knew, half the faculty carried on liaisons at some point, but the suggestion had stirred the pot. A memo with a firm statement about collegial responsibility had been issued, a copy placed in every faculty mailbox. Even though no names had been mentioned, both Rose and Jonathon had felt the sting of judgement. It rankled extra hard since their personal relationship was currently less close than even a few weeks before.

Elise lurked quietly in the background. As far as Rose knew, Jonathon had so far resisted the pull, but she was doubtful he had the wherewithal to resist if Elise turned on the sexpot siren juice full blast.

Rose figured hauling a dead animal up onto the roof of the Social Science complex constituted questionable behavior and probably violated the spirit of the memo. She mentioned this to Jonathon as he turned onto the main campus drive.

"Nonsense. This is perfectly acceptable given our professional positions and the classes we teach. We're just courteous enough to conduct the heavy lifting after hours, which in retrospect is sort of stupid, we should get some students to do this grunt work."

"True. They'll do anything for extra credit."

Getting the doe into the elevator was relatively simple. The slow trip up to the top floor was uneventful. Rose used her passkey to unlock the roof access door and they lugged the carcass across the empty hallway and into the narrow stairwell that led up to the rooftop. If their final climb up the concrete steps lacked grace, at least there was no one else there to witness their uneven progress. Once through the exterior door, they paused to catch their breath. Around them sat the fruits of their labor, white five gallon buckets distributed close to the edges of the perimeter wall so the wind carried most of the stench away.

Jonathon looked doubtful when he saw the layers of blue tarp spanning a rectangle of cinder blocks. The declivity formed in the center created a well, similar to a bathtub, which was large enough to hold the deer.

"Once we fill the trough with water, it might work," he said. Pulling the sheet of plastic they'd laid the deer on top of, across the aggregate roofing surface, he positioned it along the length of the trough.

Rose followed him and grabbed at the hind legs, swinging her end of the animal up on the concrete bricks. "It'll be a race to see if the sun decays the tarp faster than the tissue withstands the anaerobic bacterial growth. The green tarps don't break down as fast but then we have to figure out how to get rid of it too. In a way it's too bad we can't fit this specimen in the tank, the bones never clean up as nice when they're macerated."

Jonathon leveraged his half of the deer into position. "Whichever one of us gets hired can petition to increase the size of the dermestid population and build a tank large enough to process a horse."

Rose stabilized the tarp flaps with extra cinder blocks and slumped back against the wall to survey the area. Only two buckets currently held fresh occupants, a raccoon in one and a seagull in another. Ten more empty buckets were lined up against the wall near the stairwell door. To her surprise they'd found surprisingly little roadkill even though both she and Jonathon regularly haunted the roads, prepared with gloves and trash bags. In the past it seemed like she had always weighed the possibility of picking up something, but now the only thing they ran across were raccoons. They had six in the collection already and that was enough. She'd love a porcupine, an unlikely possibility in this environment, and a possum should have been common enough but they hadn't seen a single one. She'd even called animal control to ask if they had anything to offer. Once she explained their reasoning, she was invited to come in and fill out requisition paperwork. If they ever got approval they'd have a wide variety of domesticates at their disposal. She wasn't so keen about the cats or dogs the agency regularly scooped up for elimination, but the livestock and wildlife would be helpful.

Rose won the rock, paper, scissors challenge. Jonathon had to take the first water change tomorrow. Since they couldn't run the waste water through the downspouts, they relied on evaporation. During the first few days things were thick and soupy, ripe with flies and gnats. After the initial decomposition stage, topping off the water volume took on a nasty quality that even hardened veterans steeled their stomachs against.

"The price of success," Jonathon said, traipsing down the stairs behind her. He veered off toward the back exit to the loading dock where they'd parked the truck.

Rose called out a goodnight and headed toward the faculty lot. It was only ten o'clock but she couldn't wait to get home and take a hot shower.

CHAPTER NINE

The Trade-off

In an effort to avoid the cluster of students hovering near the door, Rose chose to exit the classroom from the bottom of the scaled lecture hall and sneak out through the service corridor. She'd no more than rounded the edge of the lecture podium when a student materialized at her side.

"Ms. Brashear? Can I talk to you for a minute?" The student bobbed up and down in his sneakers, like he was riding the prow of a speedboat instead of standing on a stationary floor.

"I'm just on my way off campus, Jasper." She surged forward, gaze intent on the door.

"Please? It'll take just a second. I need a letter of recommendation to apply for an emergency student aid loan. You're my last chance. Would you please fill out this form?" He thrust a sheet of paper toward her.

Her step faltered and she darted a look at the wall clock. The Fed-Ex office at the edge of campus closed at 6:00 p.m. and it was 5:40 p.m. already. She barely had time to sprint across the commons and drop the envelope on the counter. The package had to go tonight or there was no way her research proposal would make it before the deadline.

The latest rumor from Dr. Wilcox said the hiring committee wanted a candidate with research experience and that meant the best affidavits would receive priority consideration. Rose was beginning to suspect there might be a separate betting pool among the senior faculty, odds being levied on which of the runners-up would go to the greatest length. Still no word had come down from official sources indicating the position would require any special criteria, but hell, if she waited until the final requirements were posted it would be too late to find something. She decided that anything bolstering her resume could only benefit her future.

She thought she'd worked hard as a student but teaching pushed her mental and physical limits. She'd given up jogging, abandoning her regular two mile route, and still dropped another pound. Added to the eight pounds she'd already lost in the last six months, her jeans kept slipping down her hips, a sensation she disliked.

The student still bobbed like a buoy and Rose gathered her scattered thoughts. She tuned in to what he was saying.

"I know I waited 'til the last minute but I didn't know I was going to need an instructor's recommendation. I just found out the tuition check my parents sent to the college bounced and I'm about to be dis-enrolled. The registrar's office gave me enough time to process the loan application, but I'm out of options. I need to have one current faculty sign-off as evidence of my progress before I'll qualify. This lets me finish out this semester."

Rose heard the plea in his voice and wavered.

She knew the reality. Education was priced way above the ability of the student to pay. The underlying note of financial ruin in the admission that the kid's parents couldn't pay and hadn't told him, made her sympathetic. He was facing a much harder situation on the homefront than he was here at school. She took the two sheets of paper and looked them over. She'd done one of these herself years before when an unexpected tuition hike went through and she simply hadn't been able to cough up enough extra dough. The sense of panic that she wouldn't be able to finish her required coursework was a feeling that hadn't dimmed with age.

She looked at his desperate features. "When is it due?"

The boy shifted, his sneakers squeaking on the floor, looking wary. "Tonight. I have to hand it through the Burser's window before 6:30 p.m."

Rose dropped her bag on the nearest table and began rummaging. She pulled out the Fed-Ex envelope and turned to Jasper. "I'll do this but you need to do me one too." She shook the envelope for emphasis. "This has to be sent tonight. Do you know where the Fed-Ex office is located across the perimeter road from the Engineering Complex?"

He shook his head. "No, but I'll find it. If you can fill out this paperwork and help me stay in college, I'll even drive your package to the airport if I need to."

Rose hadn't thought about the late drop at the airport. She filed that bit of information away for future use and handed over the envelope and a twenty-dollar bill. "Get me some sort of confirmation. This is really important, like your future success in this college depends on this envelope making it to its destination."

He accepted the envelope solemnly.

"You've got sixteen minutes, Jasper. Move your ass."

"Yes, ma'am." He grinned and darted out the door, slipping through the throng of students like an eel.

Rose ignored the flutter of nerves in her stomach and sat down at the nearest desk, skimming over the paperwork. There wasn't a lot she needed to fill out and fortunately the student had already written in his personal information because she couldn't remember his surname. She wrote the typical phrases about how he was a promising student and needed this opportunity, looked up his scores, estimated his grade to date, and signed off on the forms. By the time she finished reviewing both pages and confirming that she'd done her part, the clock showed it was two minutes past the hour.

Jasper had either made her deadline or not.

Ten minutes later he came sliding through the door, face flushed and wearing a wide smile. He even handed back her change with the receipt. He thanked her profusely, grabbed the papers and fled in a direct line to the administration building.

With that task done and everything apparently having gone well, the moment felt anticlimactic.

She'd been toying with the idea of expanding her research and finding new sites to round out her data from Nevada. The rumors had forced her hand. It was late in the season to try and establish a field project for the coming summer, but she might as well try. Chances were good she wouldn't receive approval but at least she knew she'd done everything possible to make it happen. There were plenty of potential research sites in the west and finding one wasn't the issue. What she wanted was something that would dovetail nicely with the research she'd already completed, a locale with recognizable punch, somewhere like Yellowstone National Park.

Even though it was a longshot, she decided to go back down to the basement and make another list, maybe pore through the maps and sites Dr. Wilcox had accumulated over the years. She might find an historic site that had been documented decades ago that she could reinvestigate. A local bit of history that could be compared and contrasted with preceding research would provide a nice temporal study. It certainly couldn't hurt and going home to an empty house didn't have much appeal tonight.

CHAPTER TEN

Rose's phone rang at almost ten o'clock on Saturday night. She thought the call might be from one of her cousins but when she swiveled the cell on her bedside table and read the caller ID, she recognized Jonathon's number. She swiped her finger across the touchscreen and tapped the speaker icon.

"What's up, enemy mine?" The sound of a vehicle driving on wet pavement sounded in the background. She frowned as a pair of headlights passed by her front window. The sound and visual were too well-synced to be unrelated. "Are you sitting in your car outside my house?"

"Yeah. Come out, I need to talk to you," Jonathon said.

"It's raining and I'm not wearing any shoes. You come inside." She disconnected before he could start arguing and rolled off the bed.

The interior space of her one-room house was tight, the floorplan maximized to perfection. She unlocked the front door and was pouring water in the coffee pot by the time he pushed inside.

Jonathon looked ragged. His hair stood up at odd angles, a jarring note to his normal smooth crown. He wore blue jeans, which he seldom did, and a plain grey sweatshirt. The clothes made him look like a student. Running shoes completed the ensemble. She didn't know he owned a pair of sneakers.

Rose finished scooping ground coffee into the basket before studying his appearance. "You have to be a pod person. What have you done with the real Jonathon?"

He gave a half-hearted glare and slumped down in a chair at her kitchen table. His long legs stuck out the other side.

Screwing the lid back on the coffee canister, Rose depressed the button. Water immediately hissed and spit into the filter, the fragrance of coffee drifting in the confined space. She pulled the remaining chair to one side of the table and sat down, watching Jonathon's stiff features with trepidation. He looked pissed.

Reaching inside his sweatshirt, he pulled out an envelope and set it on the wooden tabletop, pushing it across to her with one finger.

"Don't be so dramatic. Just tell me what it is." Rose was torn between wanting to slap him and laughing.

He heaved out a sigh and opened the envelope, extracting a single page of stationary. A fancy logo, like a state seal was printed across the top. He waved it at her. "This is an official confirmation from the state of California's Department of Justice. The Office of the Attorney General has authorized the Bureau of Investigation to offer me an internship."

Puzzled by the disgusted look on Jonathon's face, she asked the obvious question. "This is bad news? It sounds pretty damn impressive to me."

He shrugged. "We were talking paid positions. Now they've offered me an internship. Hell Rose, I'm better qualified than some of the analysts running departments and they want to bring me in as an unpaid intern."

She got it now.

It was a common enough occurrence. The outside world considered the university environment to offer too much emphasis in the theoretical space and not enough experience in the trenches. There was some granular truth to the fact that lack of field expertise in crime investigation impacted the ability to read logical conclusions. Since that wasn't the kind of job Jonathon wanted, it didn't make him any less qualified to do the job in the laboratory environment.

"In that case, you should be disgruntled. They can't dangle a paid position in front of you and then expect you to jump at something that has significantly less inherent value." Her voice trailed off as he pulled out a second envelope. She raised her eyebrows in query.

"This letter is from the Sacramento County District Attorney's Crime Lab Office. It's a job offer to join the Laboratory of Forensic Sciences in the capacity of a forensic biologist." He dropped this letter on top of the first one.

They stared at the papers in the center of the table for a moment.

"Working as a forensic biologist would mean, um... not just lab work, right? You'd actually be going out to crime scenes?"

"Yes." The single word response was ripe with innuendo.

Rose didn't know the exact job description but she knew enough about working with human remains to know there was a world of difference. In the lab, everything is cleaned and processed. A disconnect exists between the crime itself and the pieces of the victim the technicians evaluate. Her own experience in working with human remains in archaeological deposits wasn't so different. Forensic biologists dealt primarily with freshly dead people. Handing the earthly remains of a child who had died hundreds of years in the past was vastly different than visiting a crime scene to review a child who had perished in some heinous act. The thought gave her the heebie-jeebies.

"What are you going to do?" Her voice was barely audible.

Jonathon shook his head, his eyes never left the crumpled sheets of paper. "I don't know. I can't make a decision."

Rose stood up and went to the counter, collected two coffee mugs and poured. She added a slug of bourbon to Jonathon's and set it down in front of him. She topped hers with heavy cream and turned to face him, leaning back against the counter.

"I'm glad you came over." She knew he disliked bourbon but it was the only spirits she had in the house.

"Me too." He sipped his drink and grimaced.

They argued the mechanics of each job offer, playing out hypothetical scenarios until they'd imagined ludicrously extreme potential outcomes. Rose grappled with getting a sense of the good and bad aspects of the positions. Eventually she dragged her laptop over to the table and they searched the crime archives, looking for cases that might provide examples of the sort of reality Jonathon would face in each job. The results were sobering.

"You wouldn't be the person talking to surviving family members, would you?" Rose asked. They'd just read the synopsis of a case pending litigation, a crime against a couple in a tiny town south of the state capital, who left behind three adolescent children.

"Doubtful. You know it isn't like you see on televised crime shows. I'd primarily be a lab geek. The only time I might go out in the field would be to follow up on details."

She refilled her coffee cup for a third time, adding extra cream to counteract the acid from the finely ground beans. "Do you know anybody on a personal level who could offer insight?"

"That's a good idea. I'll see if I can ferret out some first-hand input. Crenshaw probably knows someone." He glanced at her with a smirk. "The old guy would love a visit. He gave me an earful about preserving our friendship. Seems to think quite highly of you."

Rose snorted. "Of course he does. He wants the opportunity to take another crack at sneaking a kiss."

Jonathon flung out his hand. "TMI, Rose. The last thing I want to hear from you are details about how you cross the generational line in search of new sexual escapades." He paused and concentrated for a moment, shaking his head in sharp jerks. "No, I can't picture it."

She dissolved into laughter.

It was almost midnight before Jonathon drained his last coffee and set the cup aside. "Teaching is less appealing than working on real crime scenes, but processing data that involves survivors is daunting."

Rose thought that was an understatement and a half. "Do you want to stay here? I'll let you have the bed since you're twice the length of my sofa."

He shook his head and gathered the notes he'd made during their conversation, stuffing them inside one of the envelopes. "Thanks, but I'm going home. You should buy a new mattress. The last time I slept over I couldn't stand up straight for hours."

"That's what you get for being tall and having a spinal column designed for a quadruped."

He gave a chuckle of amusement and bent down to kiss her cheek. "Thanks for the trauma intervention."

She automatically leaned her head to accept the gesture. "I think you should postpone making a decision until at least the end of the weekend. Give yourself a chance to really absorb the possibilities. Maybe when you lay out the options and consider each route, something will come into focus."

Jonathon zipped up his sweatshirt and looked down at her. "I think I'm more into the challenge of competing with you for the teaching position than I am with wanting the actual job."

The admission didn't surprise her. As much as she enjoyed her work with students, it wasn't the focus of her professional interest. "Don't look sheepish. Neither of us is interested in the job strictly for the joy of teaching. The classroom is a byproduct of employment which allows us to complete the work we really enjoy."

"True enough." Jonathon walked across the room to the front door, pausing to look over his shoulder.

"That doesn't mean I'm not better in the classroom than you, buddy."

"Of course not," he agreed.

CHAPTER ELEVEN

The Alarm

With a professional expression pasted on her face, Rose shift-ed on the hard wood seat and waited for Mandy to get to the point. The girl had been rambling for three minutes and Rose was finding it difficult to follow the soliloquy.

"So, my dad keeps telling me I should major in something that prepares me for the real world," Mandy concluded and sent a searching glance across the table.

Rose nodded solemnly. She'd been expecting this to crop up eventually. Students only showed up during office hours when they desperately needed something. Today, Mandy was after career advice. Rose was tempted to tell the girl to suck it up and major in whatever she wanted. That she didn't need anyone else's validation to major in romantic literature or zoology, so long as she understood that the job market for graduates in those specialties was slim to hard. The irony of asking advice from an instructor who'd made that same difficult decision was never appreciated by the student body.

"I feel trapped between pleasing my parents and doing what really interests me." Mandy ended her summary statement with a dramatic sigh and slumped shoulders.

Rose related. Her own family had considered her choice of fields enough of a departure from the norm that she still encountered the fisheye glare from some of her older relatives. They acted like her interest in the past was synonymous with jumping political parties.

"Mandy, you have to understand your parent's perspective. They're thinking about the long-term. They want you to pursue a career that will provide opportunities for advancement, a living wage, and a future." Rose paused to let those thoughts sink in. The girl's parents were probably financing her education too, a serious expense. Of course they wanted to see results.

"I guess that makes sense," Mandy said.

Rose inhaled a deep breath and prepared to deliver the standard spiel. "Here's my advice, Mandy. Figure out what *you* want to do and then show your parents how it's worthwhile. What subject area will you still find interesting in thirty years? Don't choose something you'll come to despise. You'll figure out a way to make a living doing whatever it is you love. The potential income might not make you happy, but that's a different question." Mandy's lips parted and Rose held up a hand to forestall her response. The girl was practically bouncing in her chair. "Ten years after graduation you have to be able to make a living wage. Everyone can survive the starving student stage, even when it spills over into the starving young professional level, but if you select a major that only feeds your soul and not your belly, eventually you'll get tired of being hungry and cold."

Mandy looked confused.

Rose let her emotions show on her face. "I'm not going to tell you what you should major in, Mandy. You have to figure out if being a nurse like your parents are encouraging you, is the direction you want to go; or if pursuing your own interests are better."

A flurry of emotions crossed Mandy's face. Rose felt the eight-year gap in their age blossom into a chasm as deep as the Grand Canyon. "I can tell you this, there's nothing better than doing what you love, but at the end of the day you still have to pay the bills. In the medical profession you can afford more expensive bills. It's your choice."

Mandy slumped, her perfect features molded into serious lines.

There was a third option that Rose refrained from mentioning. Mandy could marry well. There was nothing wrong with being a housewife but suggesting the idea always made her feel like she should relinquish her feminism card. Mandy's lackluster interest in academic performance might indicate that a college degree was not part of her future.

"I want to major in anthropology, like you," Mandy blurted out.

Or Rose could be wrong.

After Mandy departed, Rose experienced a minor epiphany. In a moment of reflection she realized her desire to stay in Sacramento was partly about maintaining her safe and comfortable environment. She'd carved out a niche in the community and on the campus. She was content. Maybe too comfy. Was she being complacent? Was she selling herself short? The benefits of job security were many, and the close access to research sites was valuable, but maybe she should explore other options. Her course of study was winding down and she was close to acquiring her academic stripes. It would be smart to hedge her bets and apply for positions at other universities and colleges, which meant more time and energy poured in yet another direction.

A sudden wave of exhaustion filled her up. She already felt stretched too thin. The unvarnished truth was that all her efforts might not be enough. And that was enough to motivate her to wake up the computer and start searching the job listings again. She found two more potential teaching positions. The one at a community college in Las Vegas sounded especially intriguing because it kept her centered in the west and she readily fit all the details annotated that an "ideal candidate" should possess. Another positive of relocating to the desert was the increased opportunity to see her cousins who maintained a condo near the strip. She could live there rent free too, another plus. The negative of considering such a move was the leaving part and brought her back around to wanting the position in the department here.

This depressing line of thought called for an intervention.

She needed sustenance. If she left now she could stop by Tony's Market on her way home and pick up a box of chocolate covered snack cakes and a bottle of cheap red wine. A combination guaranteed to cheer her up.

Rose had just latched the office door, twisting the handle to confirm it was locked, when a giggle of laughter carried from around the corner. The sound was unexpected and eerily inappropriate for the late evening hour. Campus was a dead zone on Friday nights. Classrooms and offices sat unoccupied until Monday morning. She hefted her bag over her shoulder and started toward the corner. Another throaty trill and a scuffle of shoes brought Rose up short. The anthropology offices and labs were all in the basement, not exactly the most romantic of places to make out, but she didn't want to barge in on anyone.

The jangle of keys was clearly audible, as was the slap of a door against the concrete wall. Rose edged close to the corner and peeked around the wall. A couple leaned crazily against the doorjamb of Dr. Jenkin's faculty office, their bodies entwined. Rose wrinkled her nose. The good doctor was currently dry humping a slight figure with a moppet of blonde curls. Dr. Jenkins was a handsome man but Rose also knew her esteemed colleague was married. Since his wife was in the third trimester of pregnancy, she was pretty confident the woman chewing on the professorial ear was not the mother of his children.

The couple pivoted and stumbled back through the open door, hands yanking at clothes. Rose glimpsed the woman's profile just before the office door shut. It was Elise.

Faculty mixed it up. Rose knew you couldn't work on campus without rumors circulating about somebody doing someone, but this made her feel torn. On one hand she could just mind her own business. Jenkins and Elise were consenting adults. Then again, at some point Rose would come face-to-face with the scorned wife at a campus function and feel lousy at knowing such a secret. Of course, Mrs. Jenkins might not want to know about her husband's infidelity. Or she could not care. For all Rose knew, the couple could have some sort of hinky open marriage arrangement.

Right.

Elise was sleeping with a married colleague. So what? Yes, it was a poor decision, but it was her mistake to make. Except for that little fact about Dr. Jenkins being part of the hiring committee, Rose wouldn't really care. If the noises coming from inside the office were an indication, Elise was fortifying her position all right.

Any feeling of mortification evaporated. Rose stepped into the hallway and glared at the door. Jonathon and she had called a ceasefire in their competition, but she'd already caught him making calf-eyes at Elise from a distance. The woman in that office had broken Jonathon's heart and he was setting himself up for her to do it again. No matter how irrational her logic, the trollop was banging Dr. Jenkins and it pissed Rose off. She felt the urge to do something, she just didn't know what.

She crossed her arms and glared at the closed door. Having your faculty mentor in your pocket was expected and Elise had managed to work around that one. But having sexual relations with a second member of the team crossed the line. Rose couldn't seriously consider getting down and dirty to supplement her odds of getting hired; besides there was nobody left on the committee who rang her bell sufficiently to risk it. She looked at the elevator and then back down the hallway to the stairwell door.

Only the exterior doors were alarmed in this building. The main entrance featured a cardkey lock that bypassed the antiquated security system. After hours it was the only way in and out of the building and a faculty or staff card with the correct encoding on the magnetic strip was required to manipulate the lock.

If she took the stairs and exited out the side entrance, the building's silent alarm would trigger. Response time would be swift. The campus police kiosk was right around the corner.

Rose scurried down the hall. She was breathing hard by the time she climbed the stairs and burst out the door. The second the jamb released, the light over the door stared flashing. She sprinted around the nearest corner of the building and skidded to a halt, trying to catch her breath, hoping she looked startled rather than guilty.

Moving with a natural stride, her bag of books and papers bumping against her hip, she headed for her car. It wasn't until she reached the perimeter of the parking lot that she realized she must have gone one way around the building and the campus police had circled the other.

Coitus interruptus achieved.

At least she'd managed to disrupt Elise's evening.

CHAPTER TWELVE

The First Find

Rose crowed with delight. "I so love a good bit of roadkill. You never know when a great taxonomic specimen might be found roadside."

"I wouldn't call that one's location exactly roadside. And stop reaching into the backseat, you'll wreck the car. Besides, it freaks me out when you stroke the bones of dead animals." Jonathon slouched in the passenger seat, as much as his height allowed, and glared at her.

She ignored the sour expression on his face. "But the water staining gives them that lovely burnished brown tone."

"I can't believe you trespassed on private property to acquire the remains of a large rodent." He frowned with disapproval and pointed a finger in her direction. "It's probably a crime on multiple levels."

Rose couldn't be certain his disapproval stemmed from the fact she'd heisted the skeleton off the Water District sump pond property or if he really was annoyed with her driving. Since Jonathon's professional focus was human remains, whereas her interest was much broader and included animals, it was difficult to know where the boundaries of propriety actual lay.

"You can acquire specimens through proper channels because the college will pay for human remains when they won't cough up money for my taxonomic needs" Besides, she didn't really have any other options. Quality specimens were hard to come by in urban areas and that made the skeletonized remains of the beaver extra cool. As specimens went, it was superb.

"There's still time, you could shift your interests to anatomical investigation."

"This is as close to forensics as I intend to get. The idea is fascinating, but the raw materials of death are wet, smelly, and potentially hazardous to one's health."

He picked up on her familiar refrain. "Not to mention, exceedingly icky. I know." He grinned at her.

"As you know, I've always said I prefer my people dead. Every time I hang around your crowd, I feel the need to specify that I prefer them dead long enough to have no tissue remaining. Not to give anyone the wrong impression, since I am not so fond of dead people; but there's no arguing that a good piece of roadkill is both interesting and useful."

"I'd have to agree," Jonathon said.

She pulled over and parked the car in front of her house. The box- shaped structure lacked the charm and elegant detail of the Victorian era home to which the carriage house was attached, but she loved living in the shadow of the large house. Sitting for a moment with the car keys in her hand, she scanned the yard, trying not to appear furtive. Parked under the thick canopy of one of the sycamore trees lining the street, she couldn't see into parts of the yard. Rose hated sycamore leaves. Gloria, her landlady, loved them. She adored anything that made her feel superior to the neighbors. Her latest interest involved indigenous landscaping and since the sycamores were a native tree species, she gloated over having kept hers while the surrounding houses sported sweet gum and maples. She lectured incessantly about the importance of returning the environment to a more pristine state and just last week had started ripping out the flowerbeds to replace the perennials with more naturalized landscaping.

Rose mourned the early daffodils. She scowled as a sycamore leaf fell to the windshield of her car. The sycamores had been planted decades before by the city and, until recently,

Gloria had complained about raking the endless curling brown leaves into piles every autumn.

Rose swiftly scanned the yard again. She peered carefully into the painfully barren flowerbeds. Gloria was an avid gardener and permaculture had her in a tight stranglehold. She was an indeterminate age somewhere above sixty, a widow, and comfortably retired. She was one of the few people Rose had ever met who was actually at U.C. Berkeley back in the days of free love, heightened consciousness, and civil disobedience. Privately, Rose thought Gloria had enjoyed herself a great deal during that time, and thought it was too bad the woman had given up smoking pot because she needed some relaxation.

"Why can't we just go inside like normal people?" Jonathon asked.

Rose ignored his snippy tone. "You don't want to spend the rest of the day with Gloria, do you? If she catches sight of us, we'll be enlisted to turn soil or sent out to purchase manure. You know the risk when you come here on a Saturday."

"Good point." He slouched deeper in the seat, attempting to hide.

Her rental cottage had long been the envy of classmates and colleagues alike. Rose had been lucky enough to snag the lease during her freshman year. It was small but perfect, and within easy driving distance of campus. The only downside was Gloria. Her landlady was like one of her aunts, filled with observations about Rose's life.

Seeing no sign of the woman in the yard, Rose pushed open the car door. She pulled the plastic tote from the backseat and cradled it against her chest.

Jonathon climbed out of the passenger side, awkwardly stretching his long legs. "Why don't you buy a larger car?" he grumbled.

"I get thirty miles to the gallon. What kind of mileage does your beastly truck get?"

"Lousy enough that I have to resort to letting you drive. You know the extent of my salary." He sneered at her over his black-rimmed glasses.

"Yeah, sadly enough, I do. It's the same paltry amount as mine."

She led the way across the front yard, ascending the three steps to her front door. When she parked in back, the slope of the lot meant she stepped down three stairs. She unlocked and pushed open the door, the jamb stuttering across the floor where the century old structure had settled awkwardly. She held the plastic tote upright as her book bag slid off one shoulder and jarred her arm, barely managing to hang on to her keys. Setting her burden on the coffee table, she pulled aside a sheet of newspaper and admired the beaver skull where it rested on top of the jumbled ribs and long bones.

Jonathon followed her inside, standing with his back hunched and one hand shoved in a front pocket. With his free hand he held the grocery sack against his ribs and rolled his eyes at her.

She picked up the skull and directed his attention to the mouth. "Beaver teeth are a thing of beauty. Recessed inches deep into the jaw, they grow constantly which explains why the animal has to chew in order to reduce their scale." She withdrew the tooth from its socket, extracting the curved orange and white shape from the bone.

Jonathon walked over to the kitchen and set the grocery sack on the counter. He began unloading the contents, setting aside salad makings and dropping the package of shrimp into the sink. "You get that out of your system while I fix lunch, but then we need to figure out what to do about acquiring some larger specimens."

Rose nodded her agreement and continued to examine her find. The bones were in excellent condition. The animal had apparently lain in the same position since expiring and the remains were completely skeletonized. Bone that sits in water takes on an antique hue that looks weathered and aged, almost like ivory, and these had a lovely rich earthy color. She gloated at her good fortune. If she and Jonathon hadn't been sitting in construction traffic, bored and arguing about anatomy, she might never have glanced out the window and seen the skull nestled in the reedy bank at the edge of the pond. Her long-distance identification skills were a joke in the department but they were legitimate.

Unfortunately the water company had felt it necessary to fence the property. It was a good thing she'd worn jeans today, climbing the eight-foot chain link fence would've been a lot harder in a skirt. She'd had to load the skeleton into a plastic Wal-Mart sack that had been fluttering around on the floorboard of her car for a week. Then she'd clamped the handles between her teeth to keep the bones safe as she clambered back over the fence.

Jonathon had been no help at all, the coward. He'd huddled in the front seat of the car, sinking as far out of sight as his tall frame would allow, while she transferred the skeletal remnants to the security of the plastic tote.

"Do you have anything to drink?" He opened the fridge. "Jeeze, Rose. You should go shopping for some food. There's nothing in here but yogurt and fruit."

"That's why I had you buy groceries."

CHAPTER THIRTEEN

The Fallout

The gossip had spread all over campus by the time she arrived on Monday. Scuttlebutt was that security personnel had caught a couple of faculty members *inflagrante delecto*. Thelma Chen detailed what she'd heard about the event in swift sentences as she collected mail and ran copies, before sprinting back out the door and down the hallway.

Rose sat on the table next to the copy machine, her cheeks burning, even as a mixture of laughter and indigestion bubbled in her stomach. Her impromptu plan had been effective all right. Campus police were required to document every person present in the building at the time an alarm sounded. There were only two. The official report surely read something like "a couple of faculty were conducting a late-evening meeting", but the speculation spreading across the academic landscape sounded more like the plot from an afternoon television serial.

Elise managed to slip in and teach her morning class before word really got around. She'd have to brazen things out when class reconvened on Wednesday, but at least the first flash fire of innuendo would have passed. Dr. Jenkins had been observed entering the Department Chair's office. Rose wondered about the results of the meeting. The college didn't sanction faculty for engaging in affairs. Consensual behavior between consenting adults was a treacherous place nobody wanted to venture. Still, there would be unofficial fallout.

The next batch of news broke after lunch. As a junior faculty member, Elise was ignored. Dr. Jenkins proved a different story. He didn't receive an official reprimand. In the eyes of college officials, he hadn't technically done anything inappropriate. However, the previously circulated memo aimed at Rose and Jonathon, brought an end to Dr. Jenkins' involvement with the hiring committee.

Double score!

Dr. Crenshaw ambled into the classroom minutes after Rose let her students depart. He summarized the latest news and concluded with his personal opinion regarding the business. "It's a smack on the wrist because he besmirched the integrity of the department." He followed his words with a waggle of his eyebrows.

Rose took that to mean he thought that wasn't the appendage Dr. Jenkins should have had smacked.

He continued. "To avoid the potential for biased perspectives, he's been removed from the hiring committee. His replacement is an administrator from the Office of Instructional Services, a woman I believe."

That was interesting. Even though Rose didn't recognize the administrator's name, she hoped the new member would be less partisan to internal departmental politics.

Feeling a slight amount of guilt over the results of her impromptu decision, Rose went home directly after her final class session. The pang of consciousness weighed on her because she was usually not a spiteful person. The bundle of mail she collected from the floor beneath the mail slot offered yet another wrinkle to her plan.

Rose waited impatiently as Jonathon's phone rang. She hunched on her couch, eyeing her defunct television. She'd recently cancelled the cable service because she couldn't take any more reality-based programming and the number of post-apocalyptic shows had depleted her interest in watching television. Finally the receiver clattered and Jonathon grunted out a sound that might have been a greeting.

"Wake up. I need input."

An inarticulate rumble came across the line. "Rose?"

"Duh. What are you doing sleeping in the middle of the afternoon?"

"I worked all night." He yawned noisily in her ear. "Aren't we supposed to be frenemies, right now? Is this your latest effort to derail my success?"

She laughed at his tone. "No. It's your turn to commiserate. I got a job offer. Come over and bring pizza. I have beer, but pick up more if you're going to guzzle it like your longshoreman father taught you."

She disconnected the phone and stared at the letter on the cushion beside her. The offer had been the last thing she expected to find when she sorted mail this afternoon. Tucked between the electric bill and an insurance flyer, the creamy envelope looked important and rich. The elaborate crest in the corner above the return address looked impressive enough to belong to an Ivy League university. The institution in question was not, in fact, Ivy League, but it was a respectable small college with an impressive history of producing congressmen.

The job offer was great. Had it been one of the positions she'd applied for over the last two months, she'd be jumping with joy. She wasn't though. Michigan was low on her list of places to live, and more than that, she hadn't even applied for this position. She was ready to chalk it up to a creative practical joke when she saw the signature. She recognized the name. Information began to click together until things made sense.

She'd met Adelaide Carnarvon at a conference. They'd hit it off and spent three days drinking Irish whiskey and slaloming down the slopes between workshops. Adelaide was a department head at aforementioned college. Apparently she had an opening that needed filling and since the position was temporary, Rose needn't even undergo the task of applying for the job. That was a nice change.

Now she didn't know what to do. She liked Sacramento and the proximity to her research sites, but this new position offered a guarantee of employment in her field of expertise for two full years. Two.

Less than an hour later, Jonathon pointed a wedge of pizza in her direction and echoed her earlier thoughts.

"Moving across country for a temporary position is a big gamble." He swiveled the slice and bit off a hunk, chewing decisively while he studied her reaction. "Of course, staying here and competing against me is an even bigger gamble, so I think you should go." He smiled at her scoffing sound. "It's a good offer. If it weren't so far away and had the potential to lead into something permanent, I'd consider it. Is there any chance of that happening?"

"I haven't talked to Adelaide yet. For all I know she sent the same letter to ten other people and is just waiting for responses before she announces the candidates will have to battle it out in a televised grudge match." Rose speared a chunk of sausage with the tip of her fork.

The all-meat pizza was greasy and delicious, a good accompaniment to the heavy malt beer she'd pulled from their hiding place in the crisper drawer of the refrigerator. The three bottles were remnants of a similar feast she and Jonathon had shared after autumn midterms.

Jonathon scooped up another slice, pausing to take a bite before he spoke. "Okay, so we're agreed that the temporary nature of the position is a negative, what are the positives?" He shoved another third of the triangle in his mouth and wiggled his eyebrows at Rose.

"Well, this is where it gets interesting. I snooped around online and discovered the tenured faculty won a Fulbright and is going abroad." She pointed her fork across the table. "Why haven't we ever applied for Fulbrights?"

"Next year."

Rose nodded. "So anyhow, this guy teaches the cool classes and lets the adjunct faculty cover basic physical and cultural stuff. If I take over his schedule, I'll get to teach Magic, Witchcraft and Religion, Fundamentals of Prehistory, and get this, Anthropophagy." She leaned back in her chair, folded a slice in half and bit off a chunk, a triumphant smile curving her lips.

A frown creased Jonathon's brow.

"Let me save you from trying to remember. Anthropophagy is the study of eating human flesh. Can you believe there's a college that actually offers an entire class on the subject? It's probably the only one in the country, especially since the faculty in question is the world's leading specialist on the subject." Rose took a swig from her beer and waited for Jonathon's reaction.

"Hell, I don't know how you'll pass it up. I think you should do it just so I can tell my students there are worse things than dissecting specimens." He swallowed the last bite of his pizza and emptied his beer, wiping his fingers on a paper towel. He shook his head. "Don't tell me somebody actually wrote a textbook about this subject?"

"I hadn't thought about that. Frankly, I find mortuary customs fascinating but I'm not sure I want to spend an entire semester trying to think of ways to spin the practice into something with proper cultural antecedents."

"Tough call. You could consider this position not much different than going away to school for a few years, like doing post-doctoral work."

She nodded. "True enough. The problem is I won't have finished my doctorate yet. How much impact will it have on my ability to complete my dissertation? I can't teach a full load and still conduct research, much less write up my results in a coherent fashion. The experience would be awesome on my resume but ruinous for my timeline."

"Or possibly shoot you in the foot at any respectable university. Can you imagine the backroom conversations? Here, check out this vitae, she taught a class on cannibalism."

Rose raised her beer bottle and saluted. "Point taken."

"Get your trusty pen and paper, let's make one of your famous lists of the pros and cons."

She grabbed for the pen and pad on her desk, noting with amusement that it was the same set of materials they'd used to work out Jonathon's employment choices not long ago.

There were many things to consider, not just the subject matter which stretched beyond her normal comfort level, in moving to the eastern side of the country. There was the very real issue of continuing her research and completing her dissertation. If she were thousands of miles away it would be a challenge to continue collaborating with Dr. Wilcox on their joint study. All of her own research topics were in the west and switching gears to start a new series of projects was unwise until she had some accolades under her belt.

Jonathon slapped his palms on the table in a let's-get-something-straight gesture. "Let me repeat the advice you tendered me. Don't be rash in taking the job or turning it down. All things in life not being equal, we should just believe we have time to find the perfect opportunity, even if the ones we want don't pan out."

"That's too profound for me to grasp right now, but that's why I called you, even if you are my frenemy. You give good advice." She rolled the last beer at him. "Drink this. It's terrible and I don't want it in my fridge anymore."

He caught the bottle as it rolled off the edge of the table and twisted the lid off with a practiced motion. "Glad to be of service."

They drank in silence for a moment.

Rose enjoyed the ceasefire in the competition. If she closed her eyes and forgot about the last twelve weeks, she almost felt like things were back to normal. That reminded her of Jonathon's own tough decision. "What did you decide about your choices, between the job offer and the internship?"

He twisted the cap off the beer and belched, took another long drink and said nothing for a moment. "I rejected the internship and countered the job offer with a salary increase and laboratory equipment demands."

She raised her bottle in a toast. "Screwed your chances well and good, eh?"

He clinked the neck of his beer against hers.

CHAPTER FOURTEEN

The Emergency

A steady stream of "thanks, but no thanks" responses to employment positions arrived in Rose's mailbox. Some were letters but a few were terse e-mails. In the latter case she couldn't even hold the rejection in her hands and complain unless she went to the trouble of printing it first. Dr. Wilcox commiserated with her results, suggesting she print copies on one of the campus printers and then burn them out behind the building.

"It'll be cathartic, Rose," he said, patting her cheek before ambling off to class.

The idea had merit.

"Don't forget, you agreed to come out to the McClaskey site and give your official opinion of the historical context. I need to submit the paperwork to the Heritage Commission by the end of the week..." His voice trailed off as he turned the corner.

Crap. She'd forgotten about reviewing the site report about the prehistoric burials found at a local farm. She flipped open her calendar and scribbled a reminder note for the next day.

This had been a hard week for Rose. The official job requirements had finally been posted and included a mandate that potential candidates demonstrate their ongoing commitment to exploring new site venues. Everyone was scrambling to finalize new research locales. If Rose didn't find something soon she might have to scope out private ranch lands and contact owners who happened to live on properties containing old mining claims. There was no shortage of those in the west, but working with civilians was never as simple as dealing with representatives from various government agencies.

She seemed to be the only one facing such a dilemma.

Jonathon had locked down an unexpected FBI internship. His summer would be spent processing crime evidence in cold case files and rubbing shoulders with other throwbacks to the 1950s. The anticipation of that affiliation going on his resume had already impressed the biological sciences faculty who cross-listed his classes with the anthropology department.

While Rose was happy for his success as a friend, she was also green with envy. Even if she was able to score an internship with the National Bureau of Mines, the title affiliation didn't have the same ring as the Federal Bureau of Investigation. Not to her ears.

Elise had also scored a major coup, gaining access to the largest privately held collection of Neolithic artifacts in the United States. Then she topped that feat by receiving an invitation to visit the anthropology museum at Yale to photograph their collection of Çatalhöyük artifacts for the inventory catalogue she'd been working on in Turkey.

Rose had zip.

Well, that wasn't entirely true. She had a growing collection of taxonomic specimens, but that seemed minor in comparison to what the others would now be bringing to the table. She needed something to add to her wow factor, an association that would really impress the committee. Not only did she want to demonstrate the attributes they wanted, but she also wanted to exhibit the skills other professionals in their discipline recognized and appreciated – which explained how she came to be submitting a proposal to the Smithsonian Institution.

Aim high, they said. Well, you couldn't get much higher than the national museum complex. Her request covered the investigation of historical maps and documents, including artifact collections stemming from the historical period of western expansion and framed by the time of nation building in the United States. Her précis was broad and expansive, and beautifully written. She'd revised and reviewed every policy listed on the submissions request form, and practically memorized every hint of doctrine about how to submit requests and receive approval. She'd uploaded the file this morning before coming to campus, filing the confirmation of receipt number in her record file. Now it came down to waiting.

A headache bloomed behind her left temple. Exhaustion dogged every step as she shuffled toward the classroom. She felt like a zombie and by the glances she received from students in the hall, she must look like one too. Six more classes before she could go home and crawl back into bed. Right now all she wanted was take a dose of cough medicine and fall deep into the comatose sleep of the liquid green death.

Halfway through her lecture Rose noticed Mandy sit up suddenly in the front row. Her body went rigid and stiffened into an unnatural position. The movement was so unexpected that Rose paused in the middle of a word. Her focus turned the heads of other students. Mandy met her gaze but Rose realized there was no sense of recognition in the girl's face.

Tommy, sitting a few seats down the same row made the connection just as Rose started around the table. He caught Mandy as she tumbled forward out of her seat and lowered her gently to the floor.

Rose leaped forward and knelt beside the pair. "Mandy?"

A murmur of voices buzzed through the room. Students in the back stood up to look down the rows of seats.

"She's breathing," Tommy told her. "It's a seizure. I have seen one before." He steadied Mandy's shoulders and helped turn the girl on her side.

"Hold her steady but don't restrain her if she starts to move," Rose told him and jumped to her feet, crossing the room in half a dozen steps to grab the phone. She dialed the number for campus security and reported a medical emergency, requesting immediate assistance.

Afterward, she ushered the remainder of students out of the room. "Wait in the hall and make sure emergency personnel can get through. I'll be out shortly."

Tommy and another boy who claimed he was a friend, made sure Mandy's rigid figure didn't bang against any chair legs. A thin trickle of blood ran from the corner of the girl's mouth. The second boy saw it and raised fearful eyes to Rose.

She tried to soothe his concern. "She bit the inside of her cheek or her tongue, a minor wound."

Within minutes a campus policeman strode into the room. A short time later someone called through the door that an ambulance had pulled up outside. The EMTs came up the stairs and were directed inside. By then Mandy was conscious but disoriented. Her gaze was unfocused and her words thick as if her mouth was filled with wool but she didn't slur her words. Rose hoped that was a good sign. Within minutes the patient was loaded on a gurney and removed.

In the vacuum created by their departure, Rose pulled herself together. She thanked the students who had stayed to assist and told them to take a brisk walk around the building to work off adrenalin before returning to class. Then she went out into the hall and retrieved the rest of her students.

As people filed quietly back into the room Rose saw Dr. Snodgrass standing in the crowd beside another woman, watching events unfold.

Dr. Snodgrass released her first volley as she approached. "Taking the time to send students out of the classroom in the middle of an emergency could be construed as an unwise decision."

Rose went very still. After a night with too little sleep and weeks of stressing about the stupid teaching job, she found herself out of patience. Snoddy's unwarranted criticism, added to the general exhaustion experienced in trying to keep up with her workload, Rose lost her patience. She refused to let Mandy's health emergency be used as a wedge to undermine or question her capability in the classroom. She inhaled a deep breath, striving to recover control, but her temper bubbled over.

"I don't believe an emergency should be treated as a spectacle, Dr. Snodgrass. The students were polite enough to provide their peer with privacy."

The second woman said nothing.

"A well-managed classroom doesn't require special treatment for individuals. Mine certainly never do." Dr. Snodgrass's voice took on a chilly tone.

Rose was familiar with the woman's classroom management practices. A hardcore traditionalist who assigned students to designated seats, she didn't waste a moment of class
time. Taking roll took all of ten seconds because empty seats
were instantly identified. Latecomers would rather miss class
than arrive after the scheduled start and risk interrupting
her in mid-flow. If you accidently sat in the wrong seat, you
were counted absent that day in the eyes of the instructor.

"I've heard that about you," Rose said. Her tone indicated
the comment was not a compliment.

Dr. Snodgrass frowned.

Regardless of the outcome, Rose had reached her toler-
ance point. "The only thing wrong with my classroom management style, Dr. Snodgrass, is that it isn't a carbon copy of
yours. My generation puts less emphasis on tracking time and
more on teaching concepts. Students come to class because
they want to learn the curriculum not because they fear
they'll receive a failing grade if they miss more than two sessions. The tact and delicacy these young adults just demon-
strated in this emergency illustrates how much they care
about doing what's right and appropriate. If you have a problem putting the health and well-being of people before academic performance, then I believe you need to realign your
perspectives."

Dr. Snodgrass smiled halfway through the speech. She
waited until Rose finished speaking and then motioned to her
companion. "This is Dr. Kadamba from the Instructional Of-

fice. She's taken the last open seat on the hiring committee for the anthropology position."

At the moment Rose didn't give a shit. She looked over and nodded politely to Dr. Kadamba, but immediately swiveled her attention back to Dr. Snodgrass. At the moment the strange woman could have been the University President. Rose was past caring about politics. She was going to have her say and damn the repercussions. She took a step forward and leaned into Dr. Snodgrass' face, invading the comfortable interaction zone that most people avoid pressing inside.

"People always come first. Students should always be our priority. Academic subjects are not as important as people."

If she ever became as disassociated as Snodgrass, Rose decided she'd quit her job. Turning her back on the two women, she re-entered her classroom.

The students were very subdued.

Rose sighed out a gust of air and jogged down the steps until she reached the bottom of the lecture hall. There was no point in trying to recover her lesson plan. They'd pick up with that the next time. For now she hopped backwards and sat on the table, and began to talk. She explained without oversharing the details, how Mandy had experienced a seizure and been taken for further medical observation. She asked the class to share any information that might assist the medical staff in understanding what had happened to Mandy.

"If you know that she took medication, or had health concerns of any kind, please share that with me so I can pass along the information." She didn't think Mandy was the sort of student who dabbled in drugs, but you just never knew. Someone might be alarmed enough to share the information.

She told the class they had done the right thing and praised them for being thoughtful and respectful, especially in departing the classroom and allowing Mandy some privacy. It took several minutes for the atmosphere in the room to relax. One student asked her to explain what a seizure involved and Rose was able to direct the ensuing discussion back to the course material.

"Sit in small groups of three and discuss the various ways medical diagnosis, evaluation, and treatment vary based on cultural traditions. Start with practices in your own families and then find corollaries in the textbook."

By the end of the hour things were back on track. Rose figured she'd blown her chances with two members of the hiring committee but right now she was feeling pretty damn disgusted with her colleagues and uncertain if an academic position was really the kind of job she wanted. After today, a nice museum job sounded better than anything else. Maybe the Nevada State Museum needed a junior curator; she planned to check the job listings as soon as she got home.

CHAPTER FIFTEEN

The About-face

Rose slipped through the door leading to the roof. The two-hour break between her morning and afternoon class sessions was perfect for grading papers, cleaning the office, and changing the water in the macerating buckets. Emptying the water in the five-gallon containers required concentration. Rose didn't want to spill anything on her pants. This was her last pair of clean jeans since she hadn't bothered to do laundry in a week. It only took a few minutes to top off the water. On the days when the sun came out the buckets had to be refilled every day. Rainfall over the previous weekend had added a layer of freshness but not enough to keep the buckets filled. By the end of this week the last of their specimens would be finished. In fact, they could probably pack away the processing buckets for future use since they'd pretty much collected samples of everything in the local environment.

Pretty much out of anything new to process, Rose had put a plan in motion to acquire more skeletal material over the summer. Collecting favors from friends in Nevada, ranch hands were on the lookout for odd bones. She'd also asked if she could have the leftovers the next time they butchered livestock. It would mean making a trip to Reno to collect the raw materials and set them out for processing, but at least she'd have access to plenty of open terrain and chicken wire was cheap. If she wrapped the larger carcasses in wire shrouds, she'd have more luck keeping the small bones that often got carried away by predators. It was a catch twenty-two, since that also restricted vultures and other carrion eaters from stripping the hide off. She'd be stuck doing some additional processing but that couldn't be helped.

She immediately had offers of two domestic cattle, one bull and one cow. The sheep, goat, and horse were unexpected volunteers, as were the two pronghorn and the pig. The larger animals would make an impressive display and be particularly useful for comparison to faunal remains found in the historic sites that were regularly turned up during construction projects around town. Sacramento was an old city.

The town had grown unchecked, restricted only by the rivers, and old farm settlements overlay prehistoric villages. Already she had used animal remains on two occasions to determine historicity. The presence of saw marks on recovered bone material had indicated the use of different technology, tools associated with early intrusive occupation in the Central Valley Delta. Prehistoric peoples processed long bones by cracking them open and harvesting the nutritious bone marrow inside. Fresh bone fractured in lovely long spirals and created distinctive patterning.

Offering her expertise to help local agencies gave her a taste of what a long-term association with the university might include and it made her want the job that much more.

As the end of the semester approached, Rose ate lunch alone more often than not. She milked every hour from her schedule in an effort to find and exploit resources that might round out her experience. It was smart. Even if she didn't get this job, something she barely allowed herself to consider, everything she'd done just made her look more appealing to other offers. In addition to her already full plate, she'd agreed to proof a new article for Dr. Wilcox while he dragged his graduate students out to an historic archaeological site for a two week period. While he was knee deep in mud and muck, happily excavating a site where recent storm waters had exposed an abandoned cemetery, she was in the dungeon searching out typos. Actually, it wasn't that bad of a trade-off. The find provoked shock from residents who didn't know their expensive riverfront homes were built atop a turn-of-the-century burying ground. Also, she preferred survey and interpretation to the actual excavation process.

Contemplating the recycling stacked haphazardly against the wall, Rose debated if it were more expedient to wheel the blue cart down the hall or haul an armload of papers out to the industrial shredder every time she went to the elevator.

Jonathon popped his head through the open door and surveyed the room. "You alone?"

Rose waved him inside.

He plopped down in the chair across from her desk, propped his elbows on his knees and stared at her. "I have something to tell you."

"Don't be dramatic."

"I just accepted a full-time position with the State Crime Lab."

The quip Rose had prepared to fire back at him died on her lips. She sat up in her chair, scooting her butt back along the sculpted wood of the seat as she flailed her arms around. "What position? I thought you said they rejected your counter offer?"

Eyes shifting from right to left, his face a mask of guilt, Jonathon shrugged. "It was such a long-shot I didn't expect to hear anything. I really didn't think they'd call. Hell, it's been weeks since I sent my demands. I even told myself to go ahead and make the demands because they wouldn't call." His gaze locked on hers. "They called. They offered. I said yes."

Hands dropping to her lap, fingers twisting together, Rose studied his face. "For real? This is legit?"

Jonathon nodded.

Rose jumped up and bounded around the desk, wrapped her arms around him and hugged. "Oh my God, Jonathon, you did it. Congratulations! You really are the best of the best."

He slapped at her arm. "Quit choking me and I'll tell you the details."

They split a pack of Nutter Butter cookies from the vending machine down the hall and drank celebratory coffee from paper cups printed with suits from decks of cards.

Jonathon explained his new role. "I'll be processing crime scene materials in the lab setting but also sometimes going out into the field."

"So you'll be like one of those CSI people on television," Rose said.

He cringed. "Thanks for the insult. No. I'll be cool. I'll actually stay in my lab that looks like the cold-war-era structure it actually is and breathe asbestos-laden air while working for a meager salary and laboring my way into a retirement of paltry proportions. There will be no ravishing young lieutenants or detectives, no smart and witty plainsclothes policeman, or sexy and overeducated medical examiners. It'll be me leading a team of super-geeks who all majored in biological sciences and still game every night and all weekend."

Rose offered him the last cookie as they returned to the office. "Sounds like heaven for nerds. What about teaching?"

She craned her neck to look up at him. "All kidding aside, you're a good teacher Jonathon. Will you miss it?"

He looked uncomfortable for a moment as he swiped a hand through his hair and left it standing up in an unruly ruffled wave completely unlike his typical neat self. "I plan to officially withdraw from the anthropology position."

"At the rate the hiring committee keeps postponing the scheduling of interviews that may be an unnecessary formality."

The hiring committee had failed to post the schedule for interviews the previous Monday. Since that was the second time, rumors had run rampant. After the grumbling settled down, the general consensus blamed the delay on funding issues. There was never enough money in education and new positions were always on the chopping block.

Jonathon stopped outside the office door. "There's one other thing I want you to know. Since most of the students who take my classes are biological science majors, the biology department has offered me a night class each semester. I can still rotate course selections but that adds another two sections to the teaching pool and might impact the new hire."

This was interesting news. "Think that might explain the latest delay? They might be reworking the course load factor for the position."

Jonathon shrugged, his suit coat not even wrinkling.

"I told my department head this morning and he issued me the offer right then." He preened under her piercing look.

"Oh, all right. You deserve to feel good about the offer." She pushed the office door open and led the way inside. "There must be a valid reason the anthropology hiring committee continues to drag its feet. You're awesome, but not the reason they haven't pushed forward."

"True. They didn't throw Elise out of the applicant pool after her indiscretion with Jenkins, so my defection changes nothing much.

"That's nonsense, buddy. I'm in a much better position. Now I'm the only candidate with experience in tissue processing."

Rose stacked up the essays she'd graded and dug up the ethnographic film she planned to show during the second half of class. In the back of the cupboard, forgotten and dusty, were dozens of VHS tapes. She added transferring them to DVDs on the mental to-do list in her head.

Jonathon straightened his tie. "I hope you still feel that turning down the job offer from Michigan was a good idea."

"Call me a wimp, but I have enough trouble with freshly dead animals. People are your thing. The idea of teaching a class where the focus is all about how human parts can be ingested is, well... it just icks me out." Rose was content that she'd made the correct decision. Now that opportunity was just an offshoot of a road not taken. "The Smithsonian Institution didn't approve my application to study the collections, but neither did they actually turn it down. I'm in limbo while a committee reviews my request. Essentially, I'm right back where I started six weeks ago."

Jonathon grunted his commiseration. "At least it could still happen. Someday, maybe."

"Yeah, someday. I should have majored in some popular concentration like you did. You'll probably end up with your own reality TV show that I'll be forced to watch every week." She laughed at the horrified look on his face. "Of all the places I submitted research proposals, the only one left is the least likely to pan out."

"Yellowstone National Park?"

"Yep. Let's hope Montana is on my summer itinerary." Rose retrieved her bag and they took the elevator upstairs. Elise's class was exiting the classroom as they stepped into the hallway.

Jonathon propped one hand against the elevator door.

Rose retrieved the stack of papers that had erupted from the top of her bag. "We should celebrate our achievements tonight. Beer and pizza at your place?"

"Sure."

She surged out of the confined elevator space expecting Jonathon to move aside. He did not. She bounced off his ribcage and turned to follow his gaze. Elise sashayed down the hall, her ass swaying side-to-side like the pendulum on the grandfather clock in Dr. Crenshaw's parlor.

Jonathon's eyes were locked on the metered motion.

"Don't go there, bucko. She's bad news, especially for you." Rose jerked her chin toward Elise's departing figure. "Although you could use some excitement. It's not like you have a real personal life anyways.

CHAPTER SIXTEEN

The Administrator

Rose saw the administrator slip through the back door of her classroom just after the students had stampeded from the hall. She wondered if her morning altercation with Dr. Snodgrass was about to have repercussions. The last knot of students clustered around the podium dispersed as she contemplated if her brash words were about to blow up in her face. An official reprimand meant a nasty note stuck in her personnel file. With a mental shrug she focused her attention on doing her job.

"I'm allowing you to complete a rewrite on your essay, Adam. It is unacceptable to submit college-level work without citing sources." She stabbed a finger on his paper. "Do you really expect me to believe you knew all this information about structuralism?"

He opened his mouth to respond and she beat him to it. "Don't even try and tell me that you knew the background and personal history of Claude Levi-Strauss. Anything you didn't already know needs to be documented."

With a mercurial grin Adam snatched his paper off her desk and trotted up the stairs. "Gotcha, Miss B – I'll have it on your desk next week."

If students put half the amount of effort into doing their work as they did into challenging her authority and trying to weasel out of assignments, her job and their academic life would be so much easier.

Rose remembered the administrator was in the room when the woman descended the stairs. She offered her professional polite smile and was somewhat surprised by the warm response.

"Hello Ms. Brashear. I'm glad I was able to catch you before you left campus, I wanted to speak to you in person." She extended her hand. "I'm Rachna Kadamba."

Rose shook hands. "I suppose this is about the incident in the hallway this morning?"

Dr. Kadamba smiled. "I don't think it can be labeled an incident. Let's just say it was a professional discussion between colleagues with dissenting positions."

That was some clever rephrasing.

Rose didn't care what they called the altercation; she was more concerned with the outcome. The university system wasn't the archaic institution it had once been, but she was still a junior faculty member and Dr. Snodgrass was at the top of the hierarchy.

"Pauline was out of line. She has strong opinions and never hesitates to make them public, which is not necessarily a bad thing, but she's also a bit of a bully. I appreciate any faculty member who can stand up to her, especially an adjunct in her own division."

Rose hadn't expected praise. She stuttered out a thank you.

"I have recommended a letter of commendation be added to your employment file for placing the safety and wellbeing of the student before academics. In my opinion you're the kind of faculty member we want representing the university." She paused to indicate the front of the classroom. "I've just seen additional evidence of that sentiment. I look forward to seeing your teaching demonstration during the interview."

After Dr. Kadamba left a hard knot of nervousness instantly formed in the pit of Rose's stomach. She gathered up the student papers no one had retrieved, placed them inside the appropriate storage envelope, collected the flash drive from the computer, and tucked everything in her bag. After being lit for most of the day, the overhead projection unit buzzed and clicked as it cooled. The end of the semester was cruising up fast. She still needed to write final exams and complete her travel schedule. She'd invested so much energy into writing proposals and worrying about job-related opportunities that she felt somewhat disgusted with the lack of progress she'd made in other areas of her life. She couldn't remember the last time she'd talked to her parents or called María just to shoot the breeze.

Some of the alternative jobs she'd considered outside the academic setting sounded great but she'd discovered museum positions were even more competitive than teaching. She'd applied to three positions in the Department of the Interior. The D.I. was always in need of professionals willing to be underpaid in order to work in their respective fields. They even hired archaeologists, so an apple might still fall off that tree. She'd rounded out the cushy government positions by hitting up the Office of Historic Preservation and the Corp of Engineers too.

Halfway to the parking lot her phone buzzed with the insistent reverberation indicating an incoming text. For once she'd lucked out and found a parking place in the front row of the faculty lot; she hurried to where her car sat waiting in a puddle of light beneath one of the sodium vapor lights. Usually the trek to her car meant dodging various obstacles, some of them the homeless guys who sifted through the trash receptacles and recycling bins. A light mist condensed on the windshield as heavy fog drifted in from the river bottom. She unlocked the door and climbed inside, turning the key in the ignition just as her cell buzzed again. This time she extracted the phone and found a row of text messages, all of them from

Jonathon. He must have sent the first one while she was in the bathroom or riding the elevator up to the ground level.

Did you hear the news? Elise won a Fulbright! Part of me is proud - the rest is disgusted. Call me.

Rose whistled. She and Jonathon really needed to apply for the merit-based award program, it seemed like everybody was receiving awards for scholarship or research grants. Elise's considerable ego had just received a genuine boost. The award was an honest achievement and sure to impress the hiring committee. After a momentary pause that was only part envious, Rose brightened. Fulbrights were awarded to people pursuing goals in international locations. If that was the case, Elise would be departing for parts unknown. Rose could feel really excited about that.

She swiped at the screen of her phone again and scrolled to the next message.

Why haven't you called me yet? Elise wants to celebrate. Should I go?

Rose groaned. She'd known Jonathon was smoldering but now he'd burst into flame.

His final message made her laugh.

If you don't call me back, I'm going. You'll have to pick up the pieces again when she breaks my heart.

Rose pushed number six on the keypad and speed dialed Jonathon.

He answered on the second ring. "It's about time. Where have you been? Never mind, I don't care. You're still on campus aren't you? You really need to get out sometime and do something. Why don't you date anymore? There's still a football team isn't there?"

Rose waited until he ran out of breath. Whenever Jonathon got rattled he spoke in what she called his stream-of-consciousness mode. Every thought in his head poured out of his mouth. From the tenor of his questions she gathered he'd been considering his single status and hers too.

"I think you should go. Have fun. Celebrate. Let off some steam. Don't fall in love and for God's sakes, use condoms. Two at a time, just to be safe."

There was silence on the other end of the line.

Finally he spoke. "You think I should go? To meet Elise? Tonight?"

Rose sighed and shoved a hand across her forehead, pushing a tendril of damp hair back from her brows. "I don't want you to get hurt. I don't want your heart to be bruised. But let's be honest Jonathon, you've been pining for Elise. You know she's headed out the door, so why not enjoy her company and make the most of the weeks you have. Enjoy being young. One of us should be having sex, right?"

He made a strangled sound of exasperation and laughter. "She's not good for me but I miss her."

Rose understood. She missed having a warm lover in her bed too. "Just remember, in the back of your mind, what happens if you go chasing rabbits..."

"You did not just quote Jefferson Starship lyrics to me." A note of disgust sounded in his voice.

"I did not. I quoted Jefferson Airplane, loser. Don't call me tomorrow until the post-connubial glow has worn off. I don't think I can take that much Elise-related happiness. This does mean she's dropping out of the competition right?"

"What competition? There isn't one anymore; it's all you, Golden Girl," Jonathon said.

"I can't believe you made a bad sitcom reference. I'm hanging up now. I'd say have a good time but since you're going out with the turncoat queen, I won't." Rose disconnected on his whistle of appreciation as she parked her car behind the house.

Jonathon might harbor sentimental feelings for the dragon lady but Rose prayed he wouldn't make the same mistake twice.

The weekend stretched ahead. She had a date with her down comforter, a bottle of wine, and a brand new mystery novel. Unlocking the back door, she kicked off her shoes as soon as she got inside and dumped her armload of materials on the closest surface. Articles of clothing were stripped off and dumped in the laundry basket, clean sleep pants and a sweatshirt pulled from the dryer.

In the kitchen, she vacillated between the coffee maker and the corked bottle of merlot on the counter. Finally deciding on the merlot because the bottle was already open, she poured a glass.

The wine tasted rich and earthy, enough to remind her of a childhood visit to the Rome hillsides when she'd first tasted and disliked red wine. Leftover lasagna went into the microwave, heating while she retrieved the pile of mail from the floor inside the front door. The mailman defied physics, being capable of shoving impossibly large envelopes and magazines through the mail slot. She sorted advertisements from bills, freezing when the envelope at the bottom of the stack came into view. The logo for Yellowstone National Park was in the return address position and the subheading for the Research Division was printed in neat block letters.

She split the seal on the envelope and found two sheets of paper inside. The cover letter granted official permission for Rose Brashear to pursue research within the confines of the federal park. She'd done it. She'd gotten permission to research historic mines in one of the most biologically diverse places in the country.

Jonathon would be impressed by that fact alone. She'd call and make her announcement now except she didn't want to hear Elise's snide remark about the domesticity of her research efforts.

The second piece of paper outlined, with dire detail, the regulations and repercussions of violating the rules. She'd already read all the information when she applied for the permit, but now she concentrated on each risk. For her age and experience, she already had a lot of field experience, but being granted this access made her feel legit. And she'd done this entirely on her own.

It might not be a Fulbright, but she was damn proud of herself right now.

To celebrate, she poured a second glass of wine. She ate dinner, alone at her table, with Vivaldi playing in the background and the letter displayed against the wine bottle. It was the best meal she'd had in months.

CHAPTER SEVENTEEN

The Surprise

The semester took on a life of its own as the end of the term neared. The stack of papers that Rose needed to grade never lessened. Darkness cannibalized the hours of the day until it seemed like she never saw sunlight. Students hit the panic stage. Major assignments came due. Procrastination and fragile confidence levels brought a steady stream of sad stories through the office. Rose found herself handing out tissues every afternoon.

Jonathon virtually disappeared.

Rose spied him walking arm-in-arm with Elise and while she felt a distinct misgiving, decided the big tall boy could take care of himself.

Dr. Wilcox delivered one of Beverly's coveted key lime pies as an end-of-term present, which Rose managed to whisk off-campus before anyone heard the news and came begging.

Finally the day arrived when the interview scheduled was slated to be posted.

The morning started badly and Rose took it as a bad omen. She found a dead baby bird next to her back doorstep. The tiny crumpled form had tumbled out of a nest up high in one of the neighboring trees. She wrapped the fragile shape in tissue and buried the tiny bundle under a shrub. For someone who routinely picked up and processed roadkill, the sight shouldn't have bothered her, but it did. The premature loss of life and the sense of unfinished opportunities made her sad.

When she reached campus, the only parking place she could find was in the very last row of the lot. Spring rain showers had departed in favor of steamy sunshine. The asphalt lot was freshly oiled and the warm weather made the surface tacky. By the time she reached the cement sidewalk, traces of tar blackened the sides of her sandals.

Her least favorite student was lurking near the office door, waiting to argue about his grade yet again. She spent ten minutes going over the same ground, letting him repeat the same excuses, then she told him no and motioned him away. The Mr. Coffee maker that had provided thousands of gallons of coffee in Dr. Wilcox's office died a sudden death, complete with sparks and smoke. At least the fire alarm didn't trigger like it had the time they'd attempted to make grilled cheese sandwiches with a hot plate.

Unable to contemplate the morning without more caffeine, Rose took the elevator up to the faculty mailroom and filled her cup with the vile brew someone had made hours before. There she ran into Thelma, who wore the triumphant grin she'd been sporting for a week. She waved gaily as she trotted down the hall, a stack of research papers under one arm. She'd worn down Professor Edgestein until he'd taken her on as a second-year assistant. This event was startling enough that even senior faculty had been seen congratulating Thelma.

Rose searched her mail slot and snatched out the envelope. She wedged a fingernail under the flap and half peeled the gummed edges apart. Inside she found an announcement rather than the date and time of her scheduled job interview. She glanced at the page and experienced a sense of déjà vu. A stream of curses burst from her lips. The teaching position she had struggled and maneuvered around all semester had been retracted. Done. Kaput. Instead of worrying about refining a ten-minute teaching demonstration she was facing a new challenge. The new job listing was still in the anthropology department and it read much the same as before, with one crucial difference, the position was now tenure track.

The stakes were much higher.

Competition would expand to a nationwide search.

She considered screaming at the top of her lungs, but instead she abandoned her coffee and went in search of Jonathon. She found him in the basement lab and handed him the paper.

He read the listing.

She knew when he saw the crucial line because his shoulders jerked just a little.

When he raised his gaze, his face wore a shocked expression. "I'm sorry, Rose. There hasn't been so much as a hint of rumor." He handed back the announcement. "Look at it this way; you're still at the apex of the pyramid. There're still only going to be a handful of candidates that offer stiff competition and you've got until fall semester to prepare for the interview."

That was true.

Once the shock had passed, her brain started processing at high speed and she'd already arrived at the same conclusion. Sure, there were going to be applicants with degrees and experiences that trumped hers, but she'd already proved herself here and the staff knew the face to go with her name. People argued that wasn't an advantage but she believed otherwise. With her newly approved research locale, and the entire summer to boost the skeletal collection, she could really bolster her position. By the time interviews and teaching demonstrations were set up in September she would be in an entirely different position to sweep the competition under the rug. One thing that would really stand out would be to get something published and she knew exactly what to write and which publication to approach. If she completed her research early in the summer, she could make the deadline in time to share the accolade with the hiring committee.

After the rubbish with Elise, and the strain on her friendship with Jonathon, Rose was ready to take on total strangers. Let them come. No mercy.

Jonathon shuffled his feet and stuck his hands in his trouser pockets. "Um, there's something I should tell you."

He reminded her of a youthful Dick Van Dyke. Her grandmother still watched the reruns of the old show every evening. "Take me to lunch. Somewhere fancy and expensive so I can put the hurt on your wallet while you confess to splitting the sheets with the she-dragon."

He flushed, then scowled at her. "Are you stalking me? How'd you know?"

"I suspected. Honestly, I don't care who you caper about with, just remember she busted you up once and is likely to be a repeat offender." He said nothing. Rose didn't want to make more of production about his decision but she wanted to make certain he'd cleared the air. "I hope you told her we never..." She walked toward the door, looking back over her shoulder to make sure he followed.

"Of course. She's been nicer to you, right?" He trailed her out the door.

"Not noticeably, but she's quit scowling at me across the hall."

"That's something."

"True. I think Monahan's sounds good. We're early enough to miss the lunch rush." She enjoyed his grimace but was fully prepared to blow fifty of his hard-earned bucks on lunch. He deserved it for putting her through the trauma that would come once Elise scarpered off to wherever her Fulbright money took her. Rose considered asking what exotic locale that promised to be, but she didn't really want to know. She'd hear enough about it once they reverted to the pizza and beer stage of the healing process. If she was lucky, Elise would bug out while Rose was in hiatus this summer. Jonathon might have to cope alone. There was an interesting thought.

"You spend too much time alone, Rose. Why don't you date anymore?"

She shrugged. "I go out."

"With someone other than that old man? You know, the one who tries to kill you every time you go jogging together."

Clearly, she was not the primary focus of Jonathon's radar. She'd avoided that particular neighbor since she'd agreed to be his running partner for his sixty-eighth birthday and he'd left her gasping for breath. That had been last January.

"I'd rather stay home. I watch bad movies with you every Wednesday. You did tell the she-wolf you're booked up on hump days, right?"

He looked guilty.

Jonathon stretched his legs and caught up next to her. "Have I mentioned how much I've missed our Wednesday movie nights?"

"Not noticeably. Quit stalling. Don't make me tell her, bucko."

He wrapped a long arm across her shoulders and shook her several times. "Lighten up Rose. I know what I'm doing. I promise not to be a quivering lump when she leaves this time."

Rose said nothing but only because she bit her tongue.

"By the way, Professor Crenshaw stopped by yesterday. He said to tell you he misses you and that you should come for tea." He steered her toward his new car, an immaculate BMW which sat in the first parking place in the lot. "I think the old guy has a sweet spot for you."

Rose slid into the passenger side. She loved Jonathon's vehicular indulgence even if he refused to let her pick up any roadkill when they drove anywhere in it. "He's a good kisser."

He climbed into the driver's seat and pulled the door shut, holding up one finger. "I'm going to pretend you didn't say that and if, in some moment of complete insanity, you ever go *there*, don't tell me."

She burst into laughter. He gave her a strained look. "Oh, come on! I'm fond of Dr. Crenshaw but not that much."

He turned the key in the engine. "You say that now."

Rose thought her future looked bright, even if she was celibate. After the last four months, she'd become a confirmed believer in the idea that fortune favors the bold. She'd created new professional prospects through simple persistence. Diligence had paid off.

She felt fiercely proud of her accomplishments and empowered about her future.

Who knew what waited for her just over the horizon? Summer might bring all sorts of opportunities, maybe even romance. She just had to find out.

ABOUT LESANN BERRY

As an anthropologist, Lesann divides her time between academic interests and professional research. Focused primarily on the American west, she is inspired by the geologic features of empty landscapes. The ancient art and prehistory of those settings often feature in her work. She writes about messed-up people and sinister events, saying her stories often feature paranormal or romantic elements because life is boring without spooky stuff and warm bodies. Crossing genre lines, she pens both contemporary and historical mysteries, romantic suspense, and even a little horror.

Visit WWW.LESANNBERRY.COM for new releases.

www.ingramcontent.com/pod-product-compliance
Lightning Source LLC
Chambersburg PA
CBHW070937130626
46555CB00001B/471